"Show Me,"

Mattie pleaded shakily, "Show me about love."

"Mattie, I can't lose what you've given me. I can't lose our friendship."

"That's right, Joe," Mattie told him steadily. "You can't. It's not possible. Just as I can never lose what you've given me. We're a part of each other now. Would the loving be so different?"

Joe could not deny the gentle logic, and he didn't want to try. His eyes closed as he fought to marshal his hungering senses. "We'll do it my way." His words were achingly husky as he tacitly admitted defeat. "Slow. Easy. Soft." Emerald eyes burned into gray, searching for acceptance.

"Yes." It was all she said, but it said everything.

Joe flipped aside the corner of the blanket, inviting her into his bed. "Come to me."

Mattie slid silently under the covers beside him, shivering as Joe carefully closed his arms around her.

Dear Reader,

Welcome to Silhouette! Our goal is to give you hours of unbeatable reading pleasure, and we hope you'll enjoy each month's six new Silhouette Desires. These sensual, provocative love stories are both believable and compelling—sometimes they're poignant, sometimes humorous, but always enjoyable.

Indulge yourself. Experience all the passion and excitement of falling in love along with our heroine as she meets the irresistible man of her dreams and together they overcome all obstacles in the path to a happy ending.

If this is your first Desire, I hope it'll be the first of many. If you're already a Silhouette Desire reader, thanks for your support! Look for some of your favorite authors in the coming months: Stephanie James, Diana Palmer, Dixie Browning, Ann Major and Doreen Owens Malek, to name just a few.

Happy reading!

Isabel Swift
Senior Editor

SDRL-7/85

MARLEY MORGAN
Just Joe

Silhouette Desire
Published by Silhouette Books New York
America's Publisher of Contemporary Romance

SILHOUETTE BOOKS
300 East 42nd St., New York, N.Y. 10017

Copyright © 1987 by Marley Morgan

ISBN: 0-373-05340-1

First Silhouette Books printing March 1987

America's Publisher of Contemporary Romance

Printed in the U.S.A.

MARLEY MORGAN's

friends refer to her as a "free spirit." Everyone else generally agrees on the word "eccentric." Such is the lot of a misunderstood author, she philosophizes. Marley lives in Austin, Texas, surrounded by Hill Country and bluebonnets, and dreams of becoming the world's best hermit. When she's not writing romances, she's reading them, and devotes herself to making up endings that suit her better than the original ones.

To the dilemma I love more than all the world....

One

———

Mattie carefully adjusted the lens on her camera as she knelt behind the end zone. The game had been a wild and woolly one, and she had gotten some superb action shots as the players thundered triumphantly on the field.

The first game of a new football season, Mattie reflected wryly. And here she was, a roving photographer, an independent woman, a sensible adult, wildly enjoying the sights and sounds of a game she didn't even vaguely comprehend. As a free-lance photographer, Mattie had accepted the assignment of covering the home team's first game of the season for a state-wide sporting magazine. She had not expected to enjoy it. She had never even seen a football game before. But the crispness of the air, the smell of autumn, the roar of an appreciative and enthusiastic crowd had all conspired against her.

It was fun.

There was a feeling of companionship—safe companionship, Mattie reflected. She was with other people but lost in the crowd. Maybe her solitary existence was beginning to wear thin... Mattie shook off the uncomfortable introspection and turned her attention to the last few minutes of the game.

It was cold out today—or at least as cold as it got in an unseasonably chilly Texas autumn. The temperature would probably shoot back up to one hundred within the week, but for now Mattie watched her breath cloud in the air with a kind of childish glee and stuffed her frozen fingers deeply into the pockets of her jacket. She could not wear gloves and still retain the nimbleness necessary to capture the shots her high standards—and her current employer—demanded.

A problem she shared with the players, Mattie noted wryly, as a receiver dropped the ball. From what she had been able to discern so far, they weren't supposed to do that. Mattie's attention focused wholly on the field now. The game was winding down quickly, and the home team needed to score a touchdown for the win.

Third down and twenty-five yards to score, the quarterback, Joe What's-his-name, dropped back to throw and could not find an open receiver. Mattie watched with a kind of sympathetic horror as the defense stormed the line and came pounding toward the quarterback like a herd of enraged water buffalo.

Joe felt the pressure and, with typical determination, tucked the ball, put his head down and charged downfield. At thirty-two, Joe Ryan was the top-ranked quarterback in the league. Now Mattie and a crowd of seventy-five thousand saw why. He broke one tackle, dodged another and began to streak toward the goal posts. The excited explosion from the crowd as the quarterback stormed into the end zone tipped Mattie to the fact that this might be worth capturing on film. She wouldn't have known otherwise.

Mattie crouched in the grass and raised her camera to capture the winning—and completely unexpected—run. What Mattie didn't see, with the camera focused so intently on the quarterback, was the shove he received from behind by a defensive player.

Mattie's camera flew to the right. The football broke to the left.

The quarterback landed full-length over Mattie's body, knocking the breath completely out of her.

For a moment Mattie could not move, could not even draw a breath into her poor squished lungs. She simply lay there, absorbing the shock to her system and feeling the deep gulps of air that caused the massive chest against hers to rise and fall harshly.

Then the voice came, rumbling deep and husky from his throat, and he levered his head up to stare into her stunned gray eyes.

"Hello," Joe murmured, resting his head on his hand with his elbow planted in the grass. "Come here often?" For the moment he was too winded by the hit he had taken to think about getting up. Then again, maybe it was the soft, sweet feel of her beneath him that made him so curiously vulnerable. Whichever, he really didn't feel like moving at the moment.

In the stands the crowds were going wild. On the sidelines his teammates were celebrating. On the field the opposing players were shaking hands. In the broadcast booth the commentators were rhapsodizing.

In the end zone Mattie finally became conscious of the long, heated body trapping her to the grass, and panic rose blindly.

"Get off of me," she ordered faintly, too frightened to move, her face stiff and white with fear.

"Lady," Joe said, grinning beguilingly, "this is the best field position I've had all day. Don't ask me to give it up."

Up in the booth the commentators began to speculate. "Ryan is slow in getting up, Herb," one noted.

"Maybe he was shaken up on that last play. That was a pretty hard hit he took as he crossed into the end zone," his cohort returned predictably.

Neither saw Mattie, crushed under the sheer size of Joe's six-foot-three frame.

"That would be quite a loss for the Conquerors so early in the season, Herb. Ryan is the backbone of this team. They couldn't survive an injury that put him on the sidelines for a month or two."

The commentators fell into a lively discussion about Joe Ryan's career to date, the team's back-up quarterback and the NFL at large. Joe's incapacitation was quickly forgotten in the flurry of facts and figures.

Meanwhile Mattie began to tremble under the weight of Joe's hard body. She didn't see the smile on his face or the gentle, absorbed interest in his emerald green eyes. She only knew that she was being pinned beneath a hard, strong, *male* body, and the nightmare sprang to life.

"Get off of me," she begged sickly, with panic in her eyes. "Please get off of me." Her face was ashen white, her hands shaking and cold.

Joe immediately rolled off her.

"Oh, no," he muttered distractedly, pulling his helmet from his head impatiently and throwing it aside. "Did I hurt you? Are you hurt?"

His hands began to run feverishly over her arms and legs, searching for broken bones or obvious wounds.

It was the worst move he could have made as far as Mattie was concerned. She began to struggle wildly, viciously twisting and indiscriminately punching at any part of his body that presented itself. "No! Let me go! Damn you, let me go!"

Joe backed off enough to read the wild, uncontrolled panic in her glittering gaze, and immediately ceased his efforts to hold her still.

"Okay, sweetheart," he began in a consciously soothing tone, holding up his hands to show her she was free. "Okay, you're okay. I'm not holding you anymore. I won't touch you again, I promise. It's okay. I won't hurt you."

He might as well have been talking to a skittish horse, but Mattie, slowly coming down from her fear-induced adrenaline high, did not notice. She did not consciously hear his words, only the soothing gentle tone he had affected registered.

Gradually the trembling stopped, and color came burning into every inch of Mattie's skin as she read the incredulous, uncomprehending expression in his eyes. Oh God, what had she done? Falling apart . . . kicking and screaming like a demented banshee. He hadn't meant to hurt her, she acknowledged sickly. She had fooled herself into believing that she had gotten over the paralyzing fear, but she now realized that it was only because she had not been physically touched in years. Glass walls were always the most deceptive kind. This man had shattered hers unknowingly and unintentionally. Mattie swallowed. He would escape from the consequences, but she could not.

"I'm sorry," she managed weakly.

Joe shook his head dazedly. "No, *I'm* sorry. I didn't mean to hurt you. I wasn't trying to—" cop a feel, he completed mentally, but flinched from voicing the crude phrase aloud. Lord knew, he had frightened her enough already. Mattie scrambled to her feet.

"I'm sorry I made you drop the football," she told him with a desperate politeness.

Joe shook his head. "It doesn't matter. I had control of it when I broke the plane of the end zone. It's a good score."

Mattie nodded jerkily, backing away from his towering height. Joe took a step toward her, and Mattie tensed. But he was bending down, reaching for her camera, where it lay in the grass.

"I hope it's okay," he said gently, offering her the camera with an outstretched arm that kept the distance between them.

Suddenly Mattie's conscious mind began to function again, flooding with the details, textures and colors of the man. He was big, but she had known that already, from the way his body had covered hers.... Don't think about that! she ordered herself frantically. Broad shoulders framed a massive chest that tapered to a tight waist and narrow hips. The legs were long and hard and very well displayed in the tight uniform pants he wore. *Everything* was well displayed, Mattie thought dizzily, her eyes skittering away from that frightening aspect back to the rugged face framed by thick, tousled black hair. He had the most beautiful, *questioning* green eyes.

"I have to go," she whispered, clutching the camera to her chest.

"Wait!"

Mattie took a huge sliding step backward. "I can't," she told him shakily. "I really can't." Regardless of the speculative glances cast her way, Mattie turned and ran into the crowd of people flocking onto the field without looking back.

Only when she reached the safety of her car, her trembling fingers gripping the steering wheel, did the tears begin to fall.

And they came from a dark locked room inside her mind from which Mattie couldn't escape.

Joe stood statue still in the end zone, oblivious to the backslapping congratulations of his teammates and fans.

She was gone.

Why did he feel as if she had taken a part of him with her? He didn't even know her name! All he knew of her was what he had seen in her eyes, what he had felt in her body.

He would find her. Yes, he would find his mystery lady with the frightened eyes. She wouldn't escape him that easily. And when he found her, he would find the reason for this sudden, slashing need to see beyond her shadows and to the substance.

Joe rushed through his shower, barely aware of the postgame exuberance of his teammates. He was out of the locker room and hurtling up the steps to the network broadcast booth before any of the swarming reporters could capture him. Useless things, reporters, he thought dismissingly. Always wanting to make something out of nothing, to fashion little tin gods out of normal men. Joe couldn't think of anything more abhorrent than having his face recognized wherever he went, although some of the players in the league enjoyed it. It would offend his own deep sense of privacy to be accosted as he did his grocery shopping or jogged around the block. That was precisely why he never granted interviews. His only concession to the fame his job had brought him was the local charities to which he committed his time and money, and sometimes—unavoidably—personal appearances.

Taking a deep breath, he pulled open the door to the booth and stepped inside. Andy Butler, the anemic-looking sportscaster, was just breaking for a commercial when he spotted Joe. The red light on the camera faded, indicating the break, and Butler turned off his phony smile.

"Well, well, if it isn't the man of the hour!" Butler marveled mockingly. "What are you doing up here, Ryan? Slumming?"

Joe shifted restlessly but held his temper. "Andy," he acknowledged with a stiff nod, moving forward. "I need a favor."

Butler's eyebrows rose in astonishment. "A favor? From li'l ol' me?"

"I'd like a copy of the tape on that last play," Joe gritted determinedly.

"Collecting souvenirs?" Andy sneered. "I thought you noble quarterback types were above all that."

Joe refused to be drawn.

"Anyway," Butler continued, "you can get a copy from your coaches."

"I can't wait for the rehash of the game," Joe told him. "I need it now."

A small, manipulative smile played on Butler's thin lips. "What's it worth to you, Joe?"

Joe shrugged, resigned. "What do you want, Andy?" Joe already knew the answer.

"An interview," Butler told him with relish. "On camera. Exclusive. Now."

Joe's mind rebelled, but the image of his black-haired lady pushed him on. "All right," he growled reluctantly. "Two minutes."

"Five."

"Don't push it, Andy." Joe snared a chair and faced the camera.

Butler grinned triumphantly and signaled to the video technician to make a copy of the play Joe had requested.

The red light blinked on, and Andy began. "We have with us now Joe Ryan, the somewhat reclusive quarterback for the Dallas Conquerors and the man responsible for that last winning play." Butler turned to Joe with a congenial smile pasted on his face. "That was quite a play, buddy," he remarked, opening the air for Joe's commentary.

Joe smiled blandly into the camera. "Thank you."

There was an awkward moment of silence as Butler leaned forward, an expectant look on his face, waiting for Joe to continue. Nothing more was forthcoming, however, and Joe simply sat there, smiling benignly into the camera.

Butler's own smile slipped a little.

"You're the top ranked quarterback in the NFL, Joe," Butler continued forcedly. "How do you account for that?"

"Well, Andy," Joe leaned forward, his tone lowering confidingly, and Butler suddenly knew that something totally outrageous was about to be said. "I like to think my game is effective because I play with my brain instead of my b—"

Butler gobbled panickedly, his face pale, and Joe broke off with a roguish gleam in his eyes before finishing sedately, "Instead of with another portion of my anatomy."

"Well, Joe," Butler rushed in heartily, quickly wiping a film of perspiration from his forehead, "it's been nice talking to you. Continued success in the rest of the season. Now we're going to break for this message from everyone's favorite beer."

The red light clicked off and so did Butler's sickly smile. "What the hell do you think you're doing?" he demanded furiously, practically foaming at the mouth.

"Did I say something wrong?" Joe queried innocently, smiling beatifically. "I don't do many interviews, you know. And I *am* just a dumb jock—"

"Cut the stupid country boy act, Ryan," Butler snapped. "We both know that you were a Rhodes scholar. Take the damn tape and go."

Joe lazily got to his feet and pocketed the tape that the video technician was holding, noting absently the barely suppressed grin on the man's face. Andy Butler was universally disliked.

"Thanks for the help, Andy," he murmured laconically, and strolled from the booth.

Only when the door closed behind him did he allow a pleased, anticipatory smile to cross his hard face. His lady was captured on this tape somewhere. And someone in this stadium—another photographer, a reporter, *someone*—would recognize her.

Oh yes, he would find his lady.

"Wendall, please do something—*animalistic*!" Mattie lowered her camera to regard her model critically. "I know it's your first time, but for heaven's sake, it's not as if I'm asking you to do a centerfold!"

Wendall rolled over to bury his face in a pile of leaves. Mattie sighed and decided to try another tack.

"I could make you famous, you know," she offered idly, inspecting her nails. "Why, you could be recognized all over the world. You could be asked to do an American Express commercial." Mattie took a quick peek at her model to see how that grabbed him.

Apparently, it didn't. Wendall wrinkled his nose and blinked lazily at the camera.

"You," Mattie told him direly, "are an uncooperative rodent."

Wendall the chipmunk scurried a few feet away to corner a downed acorn, and Mattie sighed. It was better than nothing, she decided philosophically, and he did look kind of cute batting the acorn around between his paws. She lifted her camera carefully and focused. "Now, if you'll just smile into the camera for two seconds, I'll buy you a bushel bag of acorns."

Suddenly there was a smiling face in her sight. But not a smiling chipmunk face. This face was all hard masculine angles and glittering green eyes and impossibly sensuous mouth.

She was doing it again! She thought she had finally managed to banish that face from her memory, thought she had finally left it in the end zone at the Conquerors' stadium. God knew, she had tried.

After coming home from the game yesterday, she had spent a long time thinking about what had happened, somehow unable to escape the memory of the feel of that hard masculine body against her own small frame. She had looked, really *looked*, at herself in the mirror for the first time in ages, and she had easily read the shadowed ghosts in her own smoky eyes. Every inch of her delicate five-foot-two frame was trembling with the unexpected confrontation with those ghosts. Would she ever really be free of them? Would she ever be able to stop running? From Port Arthur to Austin to Houston to Denver to Dallas...to hell and back. She was twenty-three years old, Mattie thought with a sudden fierce impatience. And still she was afraid of the dark...because it was the dark that hid her ghosts, her past and her future.

Now, Mattie carefully lowered her camera and tried to blink away this latest ghost.

"I never could resist acorns." The voice was deep and drawling, and Mattie assured herself that the shiver running down her spine and curling around her toes had nothing to do with the masculine promise contained therein and everything to do with the fact that Wendall's voice couldn't possibly be that deep.

She swallowed dutifully and opened her eyes. He was still there. "Uh . . . hello."

"Hello," Joe returned gravely, his laughing eyes cataloging each feature and movement.

Mattie decided suddenly, and with great lunacy, that now was the perfect time to pretend that she had never seen this man before, that he was a total stranger who had stumbled into her view. Dismissing Wendall from her mind entirely, she screwed the cap back on her lens and took an awkward, sliding step to her right.

Joe echoed the move faithfully, and Mattie stopped, glancing quickly around her immediate vicinity of the park. She relaxed somewhat as she noted the activity around her, and the several people within calling distance. Actually, a couple of women were staring at him intently. Mattie thought it was probably because he was so huge, standing there in tight faded jeans and a white sweatshirt. The women staring knew it was because he was absolutely gorgeous.

Unaware of all this, Mattie resolutely raised her eyes to meet his.

"So," she tried carefully.

Joe smiled. "Remember me? The one who landed on top of you yesterday?"

"Oh . . . yes," Mattie murmured faintly, sounding as if she were recalling some vague distant memory of such an incident.

"At the football game?" Joe prompted helpfully.

"Yes, I remember," Mattie told him more firmly. "Are you all right? Did I hurt you?" She had a sudden, vivid mental image of being dragged into court by the scruff of her neck and slapped into prison for her crimes.

Joe grinned beguilingly. "Do you think you could? Hurt me, I mean?"

No, Mattie realized grimly. She couldn't hurt him. He was so much bigger than she was, and, besides, women didn't hurt men. Men were the master inflicters of pain.

Joe witnessed the bitter wariness cloud her eyes and wondered about it. "I came by to see if I had hurt you."

Mattie regarded him doubtfully. "How did you know where to find me?"

Joe smiled slightly. "I asked one of the other photographers on the field who you were." But that wasn't all he had asked, Joe acknowledged to himself silently. And the answers—or more accurately, the lack of answers—he had received had shaken him. He had talked to countless people before he had found one who knew Matilda Grey. Even then, the man could relay only the barest of information. She was a free-lance photographer who had suddenly appeared in Dallas six months ago—from Denver, he thought. No past, no family, no history. She worked for no one but herself, had refused offers of permanent employment in favor of her freedom. Her work was good—very good— and had graced magazines all over the country, yet she was an elusive woman. No one knew anything of her private life. No one but himself, Joe thought sadly, because he had seen into her eyes.

"So, did I?" Joe forced himself away from his silent musings to ask.

Mattie blinked. "Did you what?"

"Did I hurt you yesterday?"

Get a grip, Mattie derided herself silently. "No. No, of course not, Mr.... Um... I'm fine."

"My name is Joe," he offered sweetly. "Mr. Um is a little formal."

Mattie felt the blush that climbed her cheeks. She was supposed to know this man's name, she was sure. Wasn't he the home team quarterfront or something?

"Well, uh, it was nice of you to check on me, Mr.... Joe—" Mattie tried for a tactful exit, but was interrupted.

"Not Mr. Joe. That makes me sound like a talking horse. Joe, just Joe."

Mattie smiled unwillingly. A talking horse, indeed.

Joe witnessed the smile and relaxed. Maybe it would be all right after all. "Will you have dinner with me tonight?"

Joe saw Mattie's instinctive step backward and cursed himself silently. Smooth, really smooth. And all the subtlety of a salivating dog.

"It's only just lunchtime," Mattie stammered nervously, wringing her hands unconsciously.

"Well, of course we'll have lunch first," Joe conceded cheerfully, trying to save the situation...and the invitation. "Do you like hot dogs?" He cocked his head hopefully toward a vendor across the park.

Mattie took yet another step backward, trying to put some kind of distance between them, both physically and mentally. "No. I'm sorry, I—"

"No?" Joe nodded agreeably. "How about pizza, then? I know this great place where the pizza is so—"

"No! Look...Joe. I really can't—I have a lot to do here, and—" There had to be some graceful way out of this, Mattie thought vexedly, but her vocabulary seemed to have gone for a hike and left her stranded with this—*man*.

Joe's smile faded as he read the near panic in Mattie's eyes. What was she afraid of? he wondered tautly. She held herself as if her world were breaking apart.

"Matilda—" Joe began, but was cut off instantly.

"Mattie!" She all but shouted at him. "My name is Mattie. No—no one calls me Matilda anymore." Her voice was trembling, and her eyes were suddenly shadowed.

"Mattie is a pretty name," Joe said carefully, his own eyes watchful.

Mattie nodded jerkily in acknowledgment but said nothing.

Maybe it was time for honesty, Joe thought somewhat grimly, horribly unsure about the care and feeding of a frightened Mattie.

"Why do you think I came looking for you?"

Mattie gnawed nervously at the inside of her lip. "To— to see if I was hurt?"

"No."

She risked a peek at his face. It was calm and deadly solemn. "No?"

Joe shook his head. "Yesterday...when I looked into your eyes..." Joe sighed quietly. "Mattie, it was as if I were looking into a mirror. As if I were looking at you and seeing a part of myself." He shrugged awkwardly, uncomfortable with the baring of his soul.

"That—that's silly," Mattie derided weakly, her voice faint and shaky. "Your eyes are green and mine are gray."

"I thought we could be friends," Joe told her carefully, and saw the wall go up behind her eyes.

"No," Mattie denied in automatic self-defense. "No we can't be friends. I don't know you. You don't know m—"

Her denial broke off abruptly as she met his eyes. My God, she thought blankly. He's lonely. She could see it in his eyes, as if she were...looking into a mirror. His words came back to haunt her. He has said that when he looked into her eyes it was as if he were looking into a mirror and seeing a part of himself in her.

All her life Mattie had felt a step out of time. There were parts of herself that she knew she could never run away from, never share with another person. And because of that, because of the inherent dishonesty in giving only pieces of herself, she had refused to share anything at all. All or nothing, she thought sadly. Did it really have to be that way? Why couldn't she give just a little? Take just a little? With Joe, she thought desperately, wouldn't it be a fair exchange? They could both keep their secrets and share what they could. They would be equals, never one taking more than he gave, or giving more than he took.

"Can we be friends, Joe?" she asked in a rusty little voice. And it was all there...the fear and the hope, the desperation and the wariness, the doubt and the need.

Now was the time for restraint, every instinct he possessed screamed that at Joe. He would reach his Mattie-not-Matilda. He would know her, know the reason for the shadows in her eyes and why it felt as if she were a part of him already, but he would not hurt her in the process. He would gain a friend, he thought. He would gain a friend and lose a little of the distance he surrounded himself with. It was a more than even exchange.

"Can we *not* be friends, Mattie?"

It was a question that haunted Joe long after he snapped off his bedside lamp.

Why now? he wondered uneasily, staring blindly at the ceiling through the dark. Why her? Why after so long of feeling nothing?

He crossed his arms restlessly behind his head.

How many years of going through the motions, trying to ignore that nagging little ache that taunted him with the fear that he had nothing more to give?

Suddenly there was Mattie Grey, waiting for him at the end of that football field as if she had been waiting there all of his life. Mattie Grey, with her impossibly sweet skin and frightened eyes.

Why her? he asked himself again.

There had been women in his life. Not too many, since the only "score" Joe kept or cared about was that at the end of a football game. And never for long, because the need was surface at best on both sides. There were women who wanted the glamour associated with being seen in the company of a professional athlete and paid for it with sex and women attracted to the money he made and paid for it with insincere affection.

Had he purposefully chosen those types so that he wouldn't have to give up that intensely private part of himself to another?

He wasn't blameless, God knew. He had taken what those plastic women offered him—sex, companionship—however transient. And he had paid for it himself in the coin they sought . . . glamour, money, recognition.

And now he had found Mattie, and . . . friendship?

He honestly didn't know. What he had felt as he met her eyes that first time defied easy description. It had all the breathless shock of a helmet in the ribs, but a hell of a lot more subtlety. It was like the feel of a swim in a cold spring on a hot August day . . . and as gentle as the silken scent of gardenias on still summer nights.

Gardenias . . . yes. Mattie's scent evoked a gentle hint of gardenias and still summer nights. Somehow he knew that it wasn't the perfume she wore or the shampoo she used. It was just . . . Mattie. The scent was all her own, from those secret hollows and delicate curves he had all too briefly felt pressed against his own unyielding body.

Was he supposed to know this, feel this, wonder this about a *friend*? Somehow Joe didn't think so. He never thought about what their nose guard, Marion Dumbronkowski, smelled like. At least, at no time other than after the game and before the showers. He never wondered about the hollows and curves of his best friend's wife, Jassy Baron. Which was good, Joe allowed with a wry quirk to his lips. If he had contemplated such things, Jassy's husband, Cole, would have doubtlessly felt obligated to take him apart one piece at a time.

So it wasn't friendship he felt. Maybe, more accurately, it wasn't only friendship. Well, he would damn well *haunt* her until he figured out the whole of it.

Nothing in the world was going to take him away from those wary grey eyes and the sweetest pair of lips he had ever seen.

He couldn't walk away from Mattie Grey until he understood what it was about her that made him want to stay.

Two

And so began a wary, sometimes stumbling effort toward friendship. One thing Joe learned very quickly was that Mattie could not bear to be touched. Physical contact was threatening and frightening to her. The casual touches and automatic courtesies that were so much a part of Joe were subtly avoided with a quickened stride, a deliberate side step. At first, Joe did not consciously register her fear. Then, one day about two weeks after their truce in the park, their tentative friendship was severely tested.

They were in Joe's yard, behind the spacious home he owned in an older suburb of Dallas. Joe was raking leaves with boyish enthusiasm. Mattie was ostensibly helping, gathering up huge armfuls from the pile Joe made and transferring them to a trash bag, leaving behind a wide trail of renegade leaves on her trek from the pile to the bag.

Joe was studying her indulgently as he leaned on the rake, taking in the sparkling silver-gray eyes framed by ridiculously long lashes and the glowing sweetness of her skin, highlighted by her leaf-strewed hair. She looked like a happy wood nymph, he thought gently.

Lord, she was pretty, and so much a part of him now, after only two weeks. He felt her taking root in his life, and the sensation was wonderful. Sometimes, he felt as if they had been together forever, that he had been waiting all his life for Mattie to appear at the end of that football field.

She didn't feel that way about him, Joe knew. Sometimes the shadows in her eyes faded, but only at times like this when she could feel the space around her and the distance between them. But if she would give him time, he thought in an endless refrain that was fast becoming familiar, to show her what his friendship could mean to her, to give her the things he had been hoarding for so long.

Suddenly Mattie spoke and broke into his reverie.

"I've been reading about football." She stopped to study him solemnly over a huge armful of leaves.

Joe leaned on the rake and regarded her indulgently. "What have you learned?"

Mattie responded eagerly. "You're supposed to be arrogant."

Joe regarded her blankly for a moment, then burst out laughing. "It's not mandatory," he assured her blandly.

"And cocky," Mattie added consideringly.

"Never learned how," Joe returned regretfully.

"You're supposed to play as hard as you work and chase women—" Mattie broke off as she met Joe's suddenly penetrating gaze.

"What in the world were you reading, sweetheart? The unauthorized biography of Joe Namath?"

Mattie wrinkled her nose enchantingly, vastly relieved that he had let her earlier remark pass. "Well, all those rules and regulations and positions confused me."

"There is nothing confusing about football!" Joe defended loyally. "It is a very simple, straightforward game."

"I know, I know. You're supposed to catch the funny-shaped ball and get it into the thingamijigy."

"Thingamijigy?" Joe said, choking.

"And then the guy in the prison uniform throws up his arms," Mattie demonstrated the universal touchdown gesture enthusiastically, dumping her armful of leaves in the process and scattering them to the winds, "and that means you made a home run."

Joe buried his face in his crossed arms. "Home run?"

"Touch-up?" Mattie tried hopefully, eyeing the drifting leaves regretfully.

Joe just shook his head, and Mattie continued blithely. "But you hardly ever get into the thingamijigy. Only once since that first game," she pointed out sympathetically. "Are you not that good, Joe?"

Joe's face remained buried in his arms, but his shoulders were shaking suspiciously.

"Oh, Joe," Mattie hastened consolingly. "I'm sure you'll get better. Don't worry about it."

Joe's head came up so quickly that Mattie jumped in fear. "You stay right here," he ordered, laughing. "I'll be back in a second."

He turned to lope off into the house, and Mattie's eyes followed him all the way. More and more lately, Mattie was becoming aware of just how handsome Joe was. The envious looks she received from other women seemed to go unnoticed by Joe, but they caused Mattie to regard him with new eyes. Joe was a very *masculine* man, but for some reason, Mattie was not frightened of him—much. He never turned that masculinity toward her, never used his considerable strength against her in any way. Sometimes she forgot that Joe was a man at all—a happy circumstance, in her opinion. He was just her friend Joe, very comfortable with his own body and maleness. Sometimes, when she wasn't with him, she could think of him as the brother she had never had. That was the kind of relationship they were building—that close and that distant. It suited her perfectly, Mattie concluded happily. As for those women who watched Joe so hungrily...she didn't even want to know what they wanted of him because that caused a nagging little pain deep inside her that she didn't understand.

The slamming of the back door drew Mattie from her introspection to find Joe jogging toward her with a football in one large, capable hand.

Mattie tilted her head curiously to meet his determined gaze.

"I am going to teach you a little bit about football," Joe decreed.

Mattie jumped to her feet excitedly, eyes gleaming. "We're going to play a game?"

Joe regarded her sternly. "Football," he intoned with some degree of pomposity, "is not like Chinese Checkers. There are some rules to learn first." He trotted to the center of the yard and motioned her to follow.

"Now I'm a quarterback. Quarterbacks throw the ball." He raised his eyebrows admonishingly. "I do it very well."

Mattie muffled a giggle. She'd thought she had gotten to him with that one.

"You, on the other hand," Joe continued repressively, "are going to play wide receiver. You'll catch the ball."

Mattie studied her own slender form doubtfully. "I don't know, Joe. I'm not all that wide."

"I suppose I should be thankful I didn't assign you to play tight end," Joe muttered beneath his breath so that Mattie couldn't hear. "Okay, when I throw the ball to you,

you try to catch it, and then reach that tree—'' he pointed to a giant pine behind him ''—for the score.''

''What are you going to be doing?'' Mattie demanded suspiciously.

''I'm going to be trying to stop you from reaching that tree,'' Joe explained patiently.

''Then why throw me the ball in the first place?'' Mattie demanded with what she considered to be perfect logic.

Joe regarded her blankly for a moment, then spent the next five minutes explaining to her about offenses and defenses and opposing teams and their lack of players at the moment.

''So we have to double up, you understand?'' he finished hopefully.

Mattie told him solemnly that she did, indeed, understand. It seemed so important to him.

''Okay,'' Joe exclaimed with boyish excitement, ''let's play ball. Go out for the pass, Mattie.''

Mattie turned and ran downfield for the pass as she had seen the Conquerors do during the game she had photographed. She turned just in time to see Joe release the ball—with considerable less force than he normally did—and screeched to a halt. Closing her eyes tightly, Mattie opened her arms and waited for the ball. It was hard to tell who was more surprised when it landed neatly in her arms. Mattie opened one eye incredulously to study it there. Then, with a fatalistic shrug, she closed her arms around it and began to streak toward the pine tree and Joe.

When Mattie drew within two feet of Joe, she stopped abruptly, bared her teeth at him and snarled ferociously.

Joe was so stunned, he simply stood there, watching her incredulously. Finally he found his voice. ''Uh...Mattie?''

Mattie growled again for good measure.

"What the hell?" Joe muttered resignedly, and growled back.

Mattie feinted to the left, then the right and Joe followed, bending low for a gentle tackle. It was just the opening Mattie was waiting for. She sprang agilely into the air, planted one foot on Joe's shoulder and leapfrogged over his back in fine fashion on her way to the goal. Once there, she spiked the ball expertly and assumed a pose of lofty nonchalance.

"I scored," she pointed out with a great deal of gentleness, leaning against the tree.

Joe, from his vantage point on the ground, with a footprint on his back, eyed her disbelievingly. "Good Lord," he muttered blankly. "She scored."

Mattie danced back downfield to stand over Joe's flattened form. "Let's play again!"

Joe picked himself up from the cold hard ground in silence. "Okay," he conceded finally. "You play quarterback."

Mattie nodded agreeably, feeling incredibly calm and competent with one score under her belt, and ran to retrieve the ball. "Go out for the pass, Joe."

It was Joe's turn to trot downfield and turn for the throw. The ball bounced about five feet in front of him, and he caught it on the run. When he faced Mattie he stopped, shrugged and roared like a bad-tempered lion. Mattie was silent for a moment, then burst into peels of laughter. Grasping her sides, she fell to the ground and rolled with hilarity.

Joe studied her in exasperation. "Okay, sweetheart." He dropped to the ground beside her. "Let's establish some rules. No more growling."

Mattie nodded solemnly, tears of mirth running down her cheeks.

Joe bounded to his feet and reached down to pull Mattie up, but she ignored his hand and got up herself.

"You know, Joe, you were right," she observed happily.

Joe raised one eyebrow expressively, pretending he hadn't noticed the evasion of his touch. "How's that?"

Mattie smiled demurely. "This is a fun game."

Joe shook his head, gentle affection in his eyes. "You are a nut."

"But a *winning* nut," she pointed out mischievously.

Joe's eyes gleamed purposefully. "We'll just see about that. Go out for another pass." Joe pumped the ball once, then dropped his arm. "And, Mattie—"

She stopped running and turned to face him.

"Remember...no growling."

Mattie stuck out her tongue. "Spoilsport."

Joe laughed and threw the ball. Hard.

"Uhf." She trapped the ball against her ribs and wheezed for breath, shooting Joe a threatening glare.

Joe smiled innocently and shrugged with a "who me?" gesture. "You're playing with the big boys now."

"Big boys," Mattie muttered beneath her breath. "Huh! Big boys."

Charging downfield, Mattie came upon Joe swiftly. When she was mere inches from him, she faked to the right, but Joe was on to her and followed her dive to the left.

Sweeping Mattie, ball and all, into his arms, Joe began to trot toward his own end zone with her. He ignored Mattie's struggles as part of the game and carried her triumphantly to the pecan tree that served as his own goal.

Whirling around in a circle, he smiled down into her face. "There! Now *I* scored a touch-up. What do you think of them apples...?"

The abject terror in Mattie's eyes stole the words from his throat.

"Mattie?" His arms tightened in instinctive protection, and Mattie flinched violently.

"Let me go, please." Her voice was achingly taut, emotionless, but her lips were trembling. She seemed to be shrinking into herself, disappearing behind a wall Joe could only feel.

Gently he lowered her feet to the ground and released her from his arms. The football, forgotten by both, bounced once, then rolled to the right.

"I have to go home now." Mattie told him carefully, not meeting his questioning green gaze.

Joe's hands dropped awkwardly to his sides, and his eyes focused on her averted face. "No," he protested. "No, Mattie. Don't go. Talk to me."

Mattie shook her head jerkily. "I . . . I can't, Joe—"

"It's because I picked you up, isn't it?" The insistent tone cut across her stammered words, demanding an answer.

But Mattie was incapable of answering. She was choking on her own fear. And to think, she derided half-hysterically, not twenty minutes ago she had mentally compared Joe to a brother! He was a man—a strong, hard, *frightening* man. First, last and always. And he could hurt her without even thinking about it, without even noticing. The way he had carried her in his arms . . .

"Isn't it?" Joe's insistent voice drew Mattie's terrified attention to him. He took an instinctive step forward, then stopped abruptly as Mattie backed away like a hunted animal.

"Mattie, talk to me," he pleaded. "I want to understand."

This is Joe, Mattie reminded herself sternly. Her friend, Joe. Don't run away. Don't lose . . . his friendship.

"You scared me." Mattie's voice, when it came, was small and rusty, and her eyes evaded his.

"I was only playing," Joe told her carefully, desperately wary.

"I—I didn't know . . . you were so strong."

"Mattie, I'm a man. And a professional football player. I have to be strong." Joe felt ridiculous, defending his very masculinity, until suddenly a thought occurred to him. "Did I hurt you?" he demanded, concerned. She was so small, so delicate. Had he hurt her without realizing it?

Mattie thought about it for a moment, then shook her head jerkily. "Noooo," she conceded doubtfully, confused. "But you would have. Touching always hurts."

"Physically?" Joe probed, intent. "Do you honestly think I would ever physically harm you, Mattie?" There was a curious, naked vulnerability in his eyes, but Mattie did not look up to see it. She was wrestling with her own demons.

"I don't know, do I?" she broke out in self-directed anger. "There are all kinds of pain."

"Let's concentrate on the physical, then," Joe suggested quietly. His large hands rose to echo his words, cupping her face gently. "No . . ." he soothed as Mattie tried to shy away. "No, I'm not hurting you, am I?"

Mattie trembled delicately beneath his touch and forced herself to remain still, breathing shallowly. "No," she admitted, her voice strained.

Joe nodded, his eyes as impersonal as if he were conducting a scientific experiment. "Good. And this?" His thumbs moved to caress the corners of her mouth. Mattie instinctively drew her bottom lip between her teeth and gnawed at it nervously.

"Sweetheart," Joe murmured softly. "Don't do that." His thumb brushed against her pearly teeth and across her jaw.

"It's—it's starting to hurt," she lied breathlessly, her gaze locked on his.

Joe's fingers drifted lower, gliding against the delicate skin of Mattie's neck caressingly. "Where does it hurt, Mattie?" he probed, his eyes losing their distant expression, warming and softening in a way that oddly reassured her.

"My...my stomach," Mattie answered hesitantly, trying to identify the ache that was centered in some deep, unfamiliar part of her.

Joe smiled quietly. "Your stomach? I'm not even touching you there."

Mattie shifted restlessly. "Not my stomach, exactly," she admitted vaguely. "But—somewhere."

"What kind of hurting?" Joe asked, his eyes serious, but still with the warm gleam lurking just below the surface.

Mattie was aware that his hands continued to move on her body lightly, drifting from her shoulders and down the length of her back soothingly.

"It kind of...aches," she murmured distractedly.

Joe's hands slid softly between them, gliding gently over her rib cage, his fingers delineating each bone separately. "Where exactly did you say it...ached?" His voice was growing progressively huskier, but Mattie, in her dazed state of seduced serenity, barely noticed.

"I don't know," she managed blankly.

Joe's hands settled just beneath her breasts. "Here?"

"No," Mattie answered weakly. "Lower."

Joe's hands inched down her rib cage to settle on the slight swell of her abdomen. "Here?"

"Lower," she whispered uncertainly, dazed.

But when Joe's hands began a silken descent, Mattie panicked. "No!" she protested wildly, wrenching herself from his touch. "Don't. Oh, please don't . . . !"

Joe backed away carefully, his hands at his sides. "Mattie, what are you running from?" The question surprised Mattie as it tumbled from his lips and she jumped, despite the steady, soothing tone.

"Running?" she scoffed nervously. "I'm not even moving."

"Not physically," he agreed admonishingly. "But here, Mattie," he tapped her temple lightly but drew back immediately when she flinched. "Here, I can see you putting a great distance between yourself and the rest of the world. And in your eyes," Joe shook his head sadly. "I can see the walls go up. Every time I start to get close to you, you pull away."

"I don't like to be touched," Mattie defended tightly, on uncertain and sensitive ground.

"I know that. And we'll talk about it later."

"That's what you think, buster," Mattie mumbled beneath her breath, but Joe ignored her.

"But I was talking about a different kind of touching, and you know it."

"I don't like to be touched in *any* way," she warned him forbiddingly, chin defiant.

"You don't like to be touched—or you're afraid to be touched?" Joe demanded perceptively.

"I'm not afraid of *anything*," Mattie insisted with childish bravado. "But even if I were, not liking and being afraid are the same thing, aren't they? If you're afraid of something, you don't like it."

Joe shook his head at that convoluted piece of logic. "Oh no, Mattie. I won't let you get away with that one. Many times the things we fear are those we like—or need—the most. It's human nature."

Mattie felt cornered by the gentle, nonjudgmental logic and backpedaled furiously.

"*Nevertheless*, I don't like to be touched."

"Mattie..." Joe's voice was gentle, but his hands were trembling. "Friends touch. It's part of the friendship. I...care for you. You can't believe I would ever hurt you."

"I've never had a friend like you," she admitted hesitantly, wanting so badly to believe. "I don't know much about it."

With a solemn look on his face, Joe moved his hands to cup her face. "Lesson one, then. Friends touch—and it doesn't hurt, sweetheart. If it does, you have only to say one word—one word, Mattie—and I'll stop touching. Okay?"

"I'll try, Joe," Mattie's voice was tight. "But—"

"Trying is enough, Mattie. Right now, it's everything." His hand moved to gently brush a strand of hair from her flushed cheek. "Sometimes you seem so young," he murmured, almost to himself.

"Sometimes I feel young," Mattie replied, shrugging, carefully moving away from his touch.

Joe's hands dropped to his side. "And other times?" he probed.

Mattie drifted away, her answer muffled. "Other times I feel as old as the earth...and as dead as those trees."

It wasn't a dramatic, practiced line. The statement was curiously flat, emotionless, weary. Joe was struck by the melancholy of an unmistakable truth.

He moved to stand behind her, a beckoning support, but he did not touch her. "Those trees aren't dead, Mattie. They're just in hiding against the winter. When spring comes, they'll be bigger and stronger than ever. Stronger because they survived the winter.''

Mattie turned to meet his eyes intently. "When the spring comes...."

In the days and weeks that followed, Joe learned a lot about Mattie. They spent a great deal of time together—in between his practice sessions and Mattie's photography assignments—building on their friendship. They both treated it as a precious flower blooming out of season and requiring all the loving nourishment they could give. Each day, each hour, each minute they were together, Joe discovered another piece of the puzzle that was Mattie Grey.

Mattie was enjoying the movie they'd rented hugely... until Superman invited Lois Lane to his place. Joe chuckled uproariously, not noticing Mattie's sudden discomfort or the way her hand froze in the depths of the bowl of popcorn that lay between them as they sprawled on her living room floor. They had decided to spend a quiet evening at home. Making the popcorn had been Joe's idea and it had been fun. Half of it still decorated the kitchen floor as evidence of the food fight he had initiated.

And now Superman was putting the moves on Lois....

From Mattie's point of view, the evening was all downhill from there. She squirmed restlessly as Superman baked a soufflé with his X-ray vision, opened a bottle of champagne without benefit of a corkscrew and exchanged a hot blue gaze with Lois as a prelude to seduction. When Lois excused herself to change into something more comfortable, Mattie gave up all pretense of composure. Pushing a pillow over her face, she muttered a muffled, "Oh, my God."

Joe's eyes shifted from the screen to study her questioningly. "Mattie? Is there something wrong?"

Mattie gulped a deep, calming breath and pulled the pillow from her face. "I think I'll go—make some more popcorn!" she said desperately, grabbing the half-full bowl between them without meeting his confused gaze.

She bolted for the safety of the kitchen, thankfully missing the blatantly intimate gaze Superman directed toward his bed as he led Lois away. Joe missed it, too. His eyes were following Mattie thoughtfully.

After a moment of consideration Joe ejected the tape and trailed Mattie into the kitchen. He found her standing at the wide open refrigerator door, favoring a carton of milk with an intense scrutiny.

"Is it whispering the secrets of the universe?"

Joe's drawl from the doorway caused Mattie to jerk around in fear, slamming the door on her fingers.

"Damn!" she muttered feelingly, prying her abused hand from the door and studying her fingers in an effort to avoid Joe's probing eyes. "I was checking the expiration date of the carton," she lied blatantly, vaguely amazed at her own ability to prevaricate.

Joe's mouth twisted with distaste. "Milk and popcorn do *not* go together."

Privately Mattie couldn't agree more, but sometimes, she decided in muddled defiance, it's better to cut off your nose and bite your face. "It's a wonderful taste sensation," she insisted stoutly. She poured a tall glass of milk and grabbed a large handful of popcorn. Somehow, the two substances landed in her mouth almost simultaneously, and Mattie choked awfully.

"Argh!"

"I thought you said it was a wonderful taste sensation," Joe remarked clinically, after Mattie had finally regained control of herself.

"Not," Mattie answered loftily, "when the milk is sour." She dumped her glass into the sink and immediately followed it with the carton's perfectly fresh contents.

Joe fired a broadside. "How do you like the movie?" Mattie reacted with great subtlety by dropping the half-full carton into the sink and taking a bath in milk.

"You don't like the movie," Joe interpreted sadly, though his eyes were laughing.

"It's very entertaining," Mattie managed blithely, brushing a drop of milk from her eyelid.

Joe nodded solemnly and murmured, "I was kind of hoping we could finish that chess game we started yesterday. But if you're really enjoying the movie..." He trailed off understandingly.

"No!" Mattie all but shouted her denial, then calmed herself with effort. "I mean, no. Of course we can play chess instead. I guess you've seen this film before."

"Yes," Joe lied. "But if you'd rather watch it—"

"I'd rather play chess," Mattie insisted in desperation, missing the tenderness in Joe's eyes. *"Really."*

"Great." Joe brightened, leading her from the kitchen. "As I recall, your queen was in imminent danger of being captured...."

Mattie turned to face Joe haughtily. "My queen is gonna stomp all over your face," she informed him with chilling superiority.

Joe laughed harder than he did when Superman asked Lois to his place... and promptly lost the match.

Sometimes the things Joe learned about Mattie brought a fierce tide of joy. And sometimes he ached so much to

hold her and chase the shadows away that he felt a physical pain inside of him.

Mattie ostensibly studied the bare branches of the trees
and the boisterous children dancing on the grass around
them in the park, then sneaked another glance at Joe. He
was still doing it.

"Uh . . . Joe?"

"Hmm?" Joe was distracted.

"Are you all right?" Mattie was concerned.

"Sure."

Silence, then, "Are you in pain?"

That brought his head around quickly to meet the solemn expression on Mattie's face.

"You were making such funny faces," she explained
doubtfully.

Joe looked abashed, a little boy caught red-handed
playing doctor with the girl next door. Mattie was in-
trigued.

"Look at that little girl!" he burst out defensively,
throwing out a hand to indicate a grave-faced three-year-old
on the edge of the sand pit.

Mattie looked. The child was, indeed, standing away
from the rest of the lively crowd of children in the park.
Her eyes were focused on Joe with the sad solemnity that
only a child can produce.

Mattie understood at once. "Trying to coax a smile, were
you?"

Joe grinned disarmingly. "Without drawing undue attention to myself, yes."

Mattie nodded with calm authority. "What's called for
here is subtlety," she informed him seriously.

Joe watched with great interest as Mattie—subtly—slipped her thumbs into her ears and waved her fingers wildly beside her head.

Every child in the sand pit broke up. The grave-faced girl was rolling on the ground with hilarity and Joe was laughing appreciatively.

"Mattie, that was—"

"Subtle," Mattie finished for him succinctly.

Joe shook his head wonderingly. "You're so good with kids!"

"Some people would be unkind enough to say that's because I'm on the same mental level with them," Mattie returned wryly.

Joe grinned. "You're going to be such a good mother."

Mattie froze. She stopped walking. She stopped smiling. Joe jerked to a halt, studying her stiff face questioningly.

"No, I won't." The words were delivered in a grim, cold voice.

"Mattie?" Joe was concerned and reached for her instinctively, but Mattie shrank from his hand.

"I won't be a good mother. I won't be any kind of mother. I will never have children."

"But sweetheart—"

Mattie broke in roughly, her voice muffled. "Never, do you understand?"

Joe believed he did, and his eyes were dark as he absorbed her pain. For some reason, he thought, Mattie was incapable of having children. What must that knowledge have done to her? he wondered achingly. Did she think it changed the person she was? Did she think it would change the way he felt for her? Oh lady, he thought desparingly, is this one of the demons you fight alone?

Aloud he only said, "Yes, I understand. No children. Never."

Mattie nodded once, tightly controlled, and said no more.

And then there were the times when Joe doubted his own sanity, thanks to the crazy, cock-eyed teachings of Mattie Grey....

"Mattie, the blood is rushing to my head!"

"That's nice." Mattie was distracted, staring at her watch.

Joe was silent for a moment, forbearing. Then he said, "Do we have to do it in this position?"

Mattie regarded him patiently. "Don't be a baby. How else are we going to capture the full glory—"

"Ugh."

"Of the flat-billed platypus in his natural habitat?"

"I don't even think there *are* any flat-billed platypuses in Texas, sweetheart," Joe protested mildly.

"Not if all Texans are as noisy as you," Mattie agreed promptly.

"And why do we have to hang upside down on this tree branch?"

"Bats do it," Mattie pointed out with a total lack of logic.

"Bats have rabies, too," Joe told her blandly. "Is catching that next on our list of things to do?"

Mattie regarded him solemnly, then sneaked another surreptitious glance at her watch. "Okay," she surrendered, extricating her tangled form from the tree and standing on the ground beside his still-upside-down body.

"Okay, what?" Joe demanded suspiciously, his face bright red.

"Okay, there aren't any flat-billed platypuses in my backyard," Mattie clarified.

Joe's suspicion deepened. "Which you knew all along."

"Let's go get some coffee," Mattie suggested blandly.

Joe had no choice but to swing down from the limb and follow her departing form, berating her the entire way to the cottage.

"What possible reason could you have for making me hang upside down from a tree in your backyard for half an hour? Are you a closet sadist, or do you have a fetish for bulging eyes, or—"

"Happy birthday, Joe!"

Joe's mouth dropped open in astonishment. The entire offensive line of the Conquerors—every last single one of them—was standing in Mattie's kitchen wearing pointed party hats and standing under a banner that read Happy birthday, Sydney!

"Sydney?" Joe muttered disbelievingly. "Who the hell is Sydney?"

"That's you," Mattie answered in a hushed tone. "There was kind of a mix-up at the store, so I told the guys that Sydney was your real first name."

"You told them *what*?" Joe exploded in a muffled roar.

"Sydney Joseph Ryan," Mattie murmured distractedly, positioning a party hat on his head. "It has a nice ring to it."

Joe's eyes focused helplessly on the behemoths that were his teammates as they celebrated his birthday. Porter and Johnson were tossing an open bottle of champagne between them like a football, Kelly was kneeling at the spigot on the keg of beer in the corner and guzzling from the endless stream spewing forth, and Riley was making out with a blonde at the sink. Most of the rest were surrounding the spread of food on the table. It was chaos.

"Are you surprised?" Mattie asked anxiously, carefully keeping her distance from the rowdy men overrunning her kitchen.

Joe nodded wordlessly, wondering how to burst her bubble. "But Mattie," he finally broke out woefully, "my birthday isn't until April!"

"I know that," Mattie told him cheerfully. "But if we had the party then, it wouldn't be a surprise."

Joe swallowed in sudden fear... because he understood the logic behind her reasoning.

Three

If Joe was learning a lot about Mattie, she was learning an equal amount about him. With the appearance of Joe in her life, Mattie's very existence changed. Yet the change was so gradual, so natural, it snuck beneath her carefully built and maintained defenses, much as Joe himself had, without her notice. He had simply become a part of her life.

They spent a lot of time together—either at Mattie's small cottage outside the Dallas city limits or at Joe's large turn-of-the-century house in an older section of the city. Somehow, Mattie discovered wryly, they had ended up together part or all of every day. Joe liked to jog in the mornings, and sometimes Mattie—"the quintessential lazybones," she called herself—would keep him company on her bicycle. More often than not, Mattie accompanied Joe to practice and gradually accustomed herself to the sight of huge lumps of humanity hurling themselves at him. She even managed hesitant smiles—from a safe distance—

to his teammates. Occasionally she would meet the wife or
girl friend of a player in the stands. They all seemed genu-
inely happy and not a little surprised to meet her. "Joe's
never brought anyone to the stadium before," one of the
more forthright of them had told her. The unmasked curiosity in their eyes made Mattie nervous. What did they
think her relationship to Joe was? They were all very nice
and very friendly, but Mattie, who had spent most of her
life building and enforcing walls, had a hard time scaling
them. Only with Joe did her guard drop, and even then she
knew that a part of her was still in hiding.

Joe continually amazed her. Every day of his life he was
surrounded by people. Teammates, coaches, fans, reporters . . . and yet, as she had seen in his eyes that first day, he
was lonely. Unlike Mattie, who had carefully chosen photography as her profession because it meant she didn't have
to work closely with others, Joe's livelihood incorporated
a host of people. He responded to all of them, worked with
many of them, liked and respected quite a few of
them...and Mattie realized that none of them knew the Joe
Ryan who was her friend. It was as if he saved that part of
himself for her.

He filled needs of Mattie's that she hadn't even known
existed, and yet she wondered if she was as good a friend to
him. He was so open with her, and she stayed so closed with
him. He respected the boundaries she had set, yet he invited her into every area of his life. Sometimes, if she
watched him when he wasn't aware of it, Mattie saw something she didn't want to see . . . a kind of sadness, a yearning that she was afraid to examine too closely.

As she had told him, Mattie had never had a friend like
Joe, and every time she witnessed that sadness in him, a
niggling fear sprang to life within her. A fear that she would
lose him, his friendship and the person she was becoming.

She wasn't lonely anymore, she discovered one day, because she had Joe. And sometimes, when the past overwhelmed her, and she tried to push him away... Mattie shook her head. Joe never left her. They might be separated physically, but there was always a part of him, a warmth, a caring that Mattie carried within her.

Lesson two, Joe had told her. Friends are forever.

The game on the fourth Sunday of the season did not go well. Guiltily Mattie played hooky from her darkroom and watched the televised show. The Conquerors were trounced 35 to 7.

She was expecting the knock on her door later that evening but not the drained expression on Joe's face when she answered it.

"Joe!" she exclaimed in concern, grasping his hand and leading him into her living room. "You look awful!"

Joe managed a wry grin. "Gee, thanks."

"I'm sorry you lost."

"Are you psychic, or am I wearing a sign?"

"I watched the game on TV," Mattie told him, seating herself next to him on the sofa.

Joe winced. "That wasn't a game," he corrected her. "That was a massacre. Why did you bother? You don't even understand the game."

Mattie's eyes shied away from his. "I watched it because I'm your friend."

Joe blinked. "Excuse me?"

Mattie shifted restlessly. "Well, I don't know anything about football, and it's what you *do*. I thought I should at least try to understand."

"I see." Joe shut his eyes and turned his face away so that Mattie wouldn't see his emotion. It was times like this, when she touched him unbearably with some innocent comment, that Joe had to force himself to put some kind of distance between them.

Mattie, uncomfortable with the long silence, continued defensively. "I didn't want you to get bored with me and trade me in for a new friend."

"Oh, Mattie," Joe said, shaking his head. "You don't trade friends in like—like used cars! Friends are forever."

Mattie swallowed. Forever sounded like a long time, and she had never thought of anything in those terms in her entire life. Trying to ease the sudden ache in her throat, Mattie brought the conversation back to its starting point.

"I bet you got yelled at by the coach," she said, grinning, and poked him in the ribs teasingly but drew back abruptly when Joe bit off an agonized moan.

Her eyes met his in deep concern before his skittered away.

"Joe? What's wrong? Are you hurt . . . ?"

"I'm indestructible," he managed breezily, unconsciously placing a protective hand at his side. "I just got banged up a little in that second quarter."

Mattie pulled his hand away determinedly. "Let me see."

Joe backed away instinctively. "No, I'm all right. I promise. It's just a little bruised."

But Mattie was not about to let him get off that easily. Taking a deep, steadying breath, she grasped the hem of his sweater and pushed it up beneath his arms. She gasped as she witnessed the horrible discoloration over his rib cage.

Her eyes met his fiercely. "Has the doctor seen this?"

"Sure," Joe bluffed. "He said the color suited me."

"Dammit, it's not funny, Mr. Macho," Mattie choked out painfully. "This looks awful."

Joe swallowed as her fingers brushed gently against his skin, too conscious of her soft and feminine warmth for comfort.

"You're right," he told her abruptly, barely aware of what he was saying, with his whole being focused on the touch of her fingers. "It hurts like hell. Doc told me to rest up for a couple of days."

"Well, that's the most sensible advice I've heard in a long time," she breathed thankfully, pulling his sweater back into place. "You go home and go to bed, and I'll bring you chicken soup and tea with honey and..."

Joe shut his eyes and drew her convulsively into his arms. "You're sweet," he muttered thickly. "So sweet."

Mattie shifted uncomfortably, painfully aware of the feel of his hard chest against her breasts. Just Joe, she told herself sternly. It's just Joe. Her mind accepted. Her body rebelled.

She jumped to her feet so quickly that Joe drew a sharp breath as his ribs were jarred. "I—I'll go make you some chicken soup right now," she told him somewhat wildly, and rushed toward the kitchen.

Joe watched her go with shadowed eyes. Chicken soup, he thought grimly. Chicken soup, when what he really needed was...something he couldn't have. Settling deeper into the cushion, Joe cradled a pillow against his ribs, thinking of things he couldn't have.

He didn't even bother to lie to himself anymore. It wasn't just the curve of her chin, or the sound of her laughter, or the fear in her eyes that held him to Mattie. It was what she brought out in him, what she filled up in him. All those years, he thought a little sadly. All those years of wondering if this was all there was, of hoarding his emotions because there was no one he wanted to share them—and himself—with.

Then there was Mattie, with walls higher than the sky, but not stronger than his need. She didn't want him because he was Joe Ryan, star quarterback for the Dallas

Conquerors. Despite everything, he still wasn't too sure she knew what a quarterback was! Mattie looked at him and saw Joe Ryan. She was the first woman to see behind the image to the man. Joe didn't know if he had let her into his mind or if she had simply discarded the image as a matter of course and burrowed deeper on her own. It didn't matter anyway, Joe accepted calmly. He was vulnerable to her now. He felt her hurts as surely as she had felt his a few minutes before.

He was an intensely private man, and yet it felt good to be known so completely by that one special woman, by Mattie. It felt good to know her that way. Joe wondered if Mattie knew that when she had crawled into his soul, he had crawled into hers. He didn't think so. He felt Mattie in him because sometimes he felt her fighting to break free. He wasn't fighting to be free of Mattie. He was fighting to be a part of her.

Mattie stood in the middle of the kitchen, trembling with reaction. She could still feel the hard outline of Joe's body against her own. At first it had been bearable, because it was Joe, and he was hurt and vulnerable. Then it had changed. Some emotion buried deep inside her had trembled and glowed to life, and a different emotion had taken her in its grip. It was the old fear. Yet in a way, it was worse because it had come from inside of her, and Mattie could have sworn that she heard a wall crumbling to the ground in its wake. So as she had always done, she had run away.

Don't run away from Joe, a silent, shaky voice called to her. Don't run away from...

Sweet. He had said she was sweet, but he had said it as if he meant she was everything.

Holding that memory close, and shutting the door against that unfamiliar feeling that had swelled within her,

Mattie squared her shoulders and returned to the living-room.

"Joe, I'm sorry I—"

Mattie broke off as her eyes lighted on Joe. He had not heard a word she said. Sometime while she was fighting with her feelings in the kitchen, Joe had given up to sleep.

A little over a week later, ribs healed and the past Sunday's game won, Mattie and Joe were together again, this time in his car.

"Where are you taking me today, Joe?"

"Someplace we haven't been before," Joe answered absently.

"Well," Mattie began to count on her fingers, "That cuts out the zoo, the art museum, every park in this city, the ice skating rink—" here she stopped to rub her hip in wry remembrance "—the stadium, the reservoir, the rodeo, the sewage plant—"

"All very *educational* ventures," Joe interrupted righteously.

"Especially the sewage plant," Mattie agreed, wrinkling her nose. "My vocabulary was broadened considerably when you dropped your sunglasses into that tank."

"Mattie—" Joe began warningly.

"And then when my heel got stuck in that grid . . ."

"Well, who wears high heels to visit a sewage plant?" Joe demanded with perfect logic—male logic.

Mattie sat up straight. "If you care to recall, you will remember that I was not informed that we were going to visit a sewage plant. You told me we were going somewhere 're-fined.' You could have told me you meant refined sewage! Anyway, it could have been worse," she insisted cheerfully. "I could have made you carry me back to the car when my shoe followed your sunglasses into the tank."

"Mattie, I didn't mean for that to happen!"

"I know, you told me. You were yanking at my shoe, and it just slipped...."

"At least you weren't still in it," Joe pointed out helpfully.

"At least," Mattie agreed dryly. "All of which tells me nothing about where we are going."

"Where we are," Joe corrected, pulling up in front of a large two-story house that appeared to have been converted into some type of meeting center.

"Jameson House," Mattie read the neat sign in front thoughtfully. "A Learning Center." She turned to Joe inquiringly. "What kind of learning center?"

Joe smiled slightly. "I guess it's a place where children and their parents learn to deal with what life hands them."

Mattie considered that briefly while they both got out of the car and headed up the walk. "You come here often?"

Joe turned to her earnestly. "One of the things that I really enjoy about football is the fact that it gives me the opportunity to become involved with community affairs. This place was founded about three years ago to help children who had been 'damaged' in some way adjust to that damage. From that sprang a counseling program for their parents. It works, Mattie," Joe told her proudly, eyes shining. "I mainly dedicate my time to the kids. It's very rewarding."

Mattie shook her head wonderingly. "How did you get involved in this, Joe? And how often do you come here? Where do you find the time? What do you mean by 'damaged'? And—"

"Whoa!" Joe laughed. "One question at a time. Okay. How did I get involved? The wife of one of my teammates was killed in a car accident about three years ago. Kevin and his son were devastated. They were both so lost without Annie. That's what gave me the idea.''

"You mean you founded this place?" Mattie asked incredulously.

Joe shrugged. "Kevin did most of the work. It was a kind of therapy for him, a way to keep busy but still deal with the loss. You see, he was permanently crippled in the accident. He'll never play football again."

"So you provided the financial backing," Mattie interpreted.

"It was no big deal, Mattie," Joe murmured slightly awkwardly.

Mattie knew differently but said nothing. She understood that Joe would be embarrassed by her admiration, but in her own mind she marveled at his tireless efforts to help children.

Just the other day, she had gone with him to a local television studio, where he taped a commercial for the Juvenile Diabetes Foundation. As a local hero, he was inundated with such requests, and from what Mattie had been able to gather by the conversations around her at the studio, Joe had never refused to lend his time, money or name to any worthy effort.

She had just opened her mouth to form another question when Joe opened a door leading into a huge playroom full of youngsters. Mattie's eyes were immediately drawn to a few in wheelchairs or wearing braces, and her tender heart went out to them. Now she knew what Joe meant by "damaged." Still, the great majority of children had no apparent physical handicap, and Mattie wondered if they had—like Kevin Jameson's son—lost a parent and were trying to deal with that loss.

"Brace yourself," Joe advised cheerfully, then called out a booming, "Hi, kids!"

Mattie was caught in the middle of the pandemonium that ensued. There was a general joyful outcry of "Joe!" from a score of childish voices, then a mass rush toward their hero. Mattie almost went down in the onslaught— would have, in fact, had it not been for Joe's protective grip around her waist. Mattie didn't even think about being afraid of his touch. She just felt . . . warm.

Joe, meanwhile, was greeting each child by name with a smile and a special comment. "Jimmy, have you been practicing your pitching? One of our Texas teams is sure going to need you in a couple of years." Or, "Mandy, you got your shoes on the right feet! But I see you saved me the honor of lacing them up, at least." And, to one of the children in a wheelchair, "Tomas, I hear you've got that chair doing wheelies and burning rubber. Practicing for the Indy 500?"

The children plainly adored him. Mattie felt her heart melting and forming a puddle at her feet. He had probably spent his whole life healing birds with broken wings in one form or another.

Mattie turned away to scan the room with intense interest. She inched closer to Joe to make herself heard over the excited babble of children hanging on him.

"She doesn't appear to have joined your fan club." Mattie nodded to a little girl, perhaps seven or eight years old, who sat alone on the opposite side of the room. She exhibited no interest in their arrival, not even raising her eyes to them. It was as though she were in a separate room and alone within its walls.

"That's Janie." Joe's voice was steady, but grim enough to draw Mattie's eyes to his face questioningly. There she saw the tightness of his jaw and a kind of fierce anger banked in his eyes. "And no, I wouldn't say she's a fan of mine—or any man."

"Is she a problem child?" Mattie probed tentatively.

"No more than she's been forced to be," Joe answered enigmatically.

"What do you mean?"

Joe did not immediately answer. Instead he bent down to the clutch of children surrounding them and instructed them to choose sides for what was evidently a well-worn tradition when Joe visited—a football game. They went scurrying outside with shrieks of joy. Only then did Joe turn back to face Mattie.

"Joe...?"

"Janie was sexually abused by her father from the time she was four years old," he told her with a kind of restrained grimness that only served to emphasize his fury. "She does not communicate well with people as a result of that abuse. She is terrified of men in general, and perhaps me more than most, they tell me, because of my size." Joe's tone, if possible, became even grimmer. "Her father was evidently my height and weight, so naturally she feels I'm going to hurt her the way that bastard did."

There was real pain in Joe's voice, but Mattie, pale and trembling, barely heard it.

"Her father?" she repeated hoarsely. "Her own father did—that to her?"

"Janie's mother finally found out what was going on," Joe continued flatly. "Oh, not because Janie told her—the scum told Janie her mother would be angry with her if she found out that he loved Janie more than he loved her mother. Janie's mother just came home unexpectedly, and—" Joe broke off in disgust, his eyes focused on Janie across the room. "They divorced. Janie's mother was brave enough—or foolish enough—to press charges. He was convicted, and now on top of everything else, Janie lives with the fact that her father is in prison because of her. At

least, that's how she sees it. There are no winners in a situation like that, just losers. They lost all the way around.
Janie lost a father, her mother lost a husband, and he killed
something inside of that child that could have been so
beautiful—''

Joe broke off abruptly as his eyes moved from Janie to
Mattie. Her face was white, completely drained of color,
and her lips, pressed tightly together to prevent them from
trembling, were bloodless.

"Mattie! Are you all right? You look like you're going
to faint." His arm moved to support her but dropped immediately as she struggled from his hold.

"Mattie?" Joe's voice was wary now. It had been a long
time since Mattie had flinched from his touch. Not since the
evening he had come to her cottage after losing the game
had she run from him. What hell was she revisiting now?

"I'm fine," Mattie answered, her voice strained and
pathetically unconvincing as she tore her eyes from Janie's
hunched little figure to meet Joe's concerned gaze. "I'm
fine. Let's go meet some of these kids of yours. They seem
like a pretty lively bunch." She all but ran outside after the
children and never looked toward Janie.

Joe studied her stiff back with grave eyes, then turned to
look at Janie. What had Mattie seen that had frightened her
so?

It was more than thirty minutes later when Joe emerged
from a cheerful and highly competitive football game and
noticed that Mattie was no longer cheering both teams on
from the sidelines. With a pang of concern, he searched the
yard for her. Where could she be? A change of quarterback was quickly accomplished, and Joe slipped away from
the rowdy contest.

He found her in the playroom, sitting across from Janie. They were separated by a table, not touching, not talking to each other, although Mattie's voice could be heard as she contemplated the child's puzzle in front of her.

"No... that won't fit there. But if I move it here—" her hand shifted the puzzle piece to another corner "—then I can't put this here." She frowned and rested her chin on her hands. She had obviously been working at this for a while.

Neither moved for a long moment, and Joe, from his position in the doorway, had the impression that Mattie was holding her breath. Then slowly, very slowly, Janie slid toward the puzzle and silently fit the pieces together.

"Hey, no fair! I bet you've done this puzzle before."

Janie's eyes rose to meet Mattie's with a small, tentative smile in their depths. But the smile died instantly as her eyes lighted on Joe in the doorway.

Joe could almost feel her withdrawal and flinched inwardly. Mattie swung around to locate the cause.

"Joe! I thought you were playing football."

Joe shifted awkwardly in the doorway, wanting to stay but torn by the need to leave and erase the swift fear in Janie's eyes. Mattie read the situation quickly. Drawing a deep, steadying breath, she rose and walked to Joe's side, then took his hand in hers. She felt that strange bolt of emotion that was becoming fearfully familiar to her but refused to drop his hand under Janie's watchful gaze.

"Janie, this is my friend, Joe. Have you met him?"

Janie watched with wary eyes as they drew closer, but said nothing, studying their clasped hands.

"Hi, Janie," Joe tried tentatively, his tone gentle.

Janie did not answer, did not even appear to hear him as her eyes fixed on some object over his left shoulder.

The tension in the room was thick, and Joe's hands tightened unconsciously around Mattie's, crushing the delicate bones. She flinched involuntarily, a small cry forced from her lips, and Janie's head snapped around. She saw the pain in Mattie's face and began to tremble, sliding back on the floor. Tears poured from her eyes, yet she made no sound. Her gaze was locked on Joe in abject terror, and Mattie flinched at the sight. It was the same look an animal, dying of abuse, cast its tormentor, and in a child it was agony to witness.

Although Joe had released Mattie's hand instantly when she had cried out, he could not move. He was frozen to the spot as he witnessed Janie's terror.

"Joe, go find her mother. Find a counselor."

Joe simply stood there, agonized, and Mattie grabbed his arm and shook him. "Go *now*, Joe."

Joe bolted from the room, and Mattie turned to Janie with a soothing word.

But she knew that no words would ever erase the horror in Janie's mind.

The drive home passed in total silence. Janie's mother had eventually calmed the little girl down and assured Joe that he wasn't to blame himself for her reaction. Despite those reassurances, the stricken expression had not left Joe's face, and it remained there now. Mattie didn't know what to do to take that look out of his eyes, so she remained silent and helpless.

It wasn't until they pulled up in front of Mattie's cottage that Joe spoke. His hands were wrapped tightly around the steering wheel, and he stared straight ahead with blank eyes.

"The fear in her eyes," he said softly. "Did you see it, Mattie?"

"Yes."

"I put that fear there."

"No," Mattie said, denying the bitter self-accusation. "No, Joe. Her father put the fear there. You just—got in the way."

Joe made a bitter sound at the back of his throat and turned to face her. "Got in the way. Yeah . . . I wanted to help her," he burst out with sudden emotion. "I just wanted to help her, to show her that not all men would . . . and instead I confirmed all those fears."

"Joe, you're being too hard on yourself." Mattie tried to console him.

"Am I?" Joe questioned disbelievingly. "I scared Janie to death. I hurt you—I didn't mean to hurt you, Mattie."

Mattie put one small hand over his on the steering wheel in silent acknowledgement. She knew it would do no good to protest that he hadn't hurt her. She could see the self-condemnation in his eyes.

"You seemed to be getting along so well with her before I broke in." Joe's eyes lit with enthusiasm. "You really seemed to be reaching her. Maybe you could come back with me next week and . . ."

"No." Mattie's arms crossed her body in instinctive protection.

"No?" Joe echoed disbelievingly. "But, Mattie, you could help her, I know you could."

"No, please Joe. Don't force this. I can't help Janie. I really can't." She reached for the handle to release the door, but Joe caught her before she could escape.

"Mattie, what are you afraid of? What are you running from now?"

Mattie shook off his hand. "Joe, I admire what you're doing at Jameson House. I really do. And I would like to go back with you sometime. But I can't help Janie. Don't ask that of me."

She had that look in her eyes again, Joe thought bleakly. The one that said she was being chased by a not-so-distant ghost. Joe studied her white face uncomprehendingly. He had pushed against her stony walls and come away battered and confused—again. Would he ever be able to scale their heights?

Mattie winced as yet another linebacker piled onto the stack on top of Joe. Holding her breath, she waited for him to roll out from beneath the human tonnage as he had done all during this practice session. He had tried to explain to her why such sessions were important—something to do with learning to hang on to the ball when he was sacked, which to Mattie sounded like something that was done to groceries, not people. Despite the explanation, Mattie still could not help feeling that if Joe were going to be buried under several tons of hulking linebackers, it would be infinitely preferable if he only had to go through it once a week—on game day—rather than at practice, too. Joe had agreed wholeheartedly and invited her to discuss her theories with the coach. Mattie declined and settled in to watch him get pounded to the ground by his teammates and friends.

"Okay, guys, hit the showers!" Mattie looked up as she heard the coach clear the players from the field. Joe began to jog to the stand where Mattie waited but was pulled up by the coach's bellow. "Joe! You really didn't get time to practice the long ball. Take thirty minutes now."

Joe's eyes met Mattie's wryly, and she smiled back.

"Sure, coach," Joe called obligingly.

Coach Rusky nodded once and followed the rest of the team off the field.

Joe waited until he was out of sight and crossed to Mattie dejectedly. "Let's go," he suggested hopefully.

Mattie shook her head. "You'll get fined. Again."

"But I'm hungry," Joe muttered, looking like a sulky little boy.

"You've already contributed a couple of thousand to the team coffers," Mattie pointed out. "There was that time you skipped practice to go on that assignment with me...."

"I didn't want you to get lonely," Joe protested mildly.

"And the time you threw the game ball into the stands...."

"The little boy was in a wheelchair, Mattie. You should have seen the way his eyes lit up when he caught that ball."

"I did, Joe," Mattie told him tenderly. "I watched that game on TV, remember?"

"Okay, okay," Joe gave in with good humor. "Another thirty minutes. Think you can hold out?"

"Sure." Mattie waved her camera at him. "I never get bored with old Sam here for company."

"Sam?" Joe repeated blankly, peering at the camera suspiciously. "I thought that one was Daisy?"

Mattie sighed in mock exasperation. "Daisy is the Nikon."

"Oh." Joe looked properly subdued, then sneaked a glance at her watch and brightened. "Only twenty-seven minutes now."

Mattie laughed. "Go throw your long balls."

"Come run them down for me," he wheedled hopefully.

Mattie looked around the field. Not a soul in sight. "Okay." She set down the camera she had been using—taking pictures was as much a part of her as breathing and Joe had become her favorite subject—and started for the stairs that led to the field on the other side of the stands.

"Here, I'll help you over the fence," Joe offered, holding his arms out invitingly.

Mattie hesitated for one second before moving into reach. Joe gripped either side of her waist gently and swung her effortlessly over the iron bars and down to the field. Mattie's hands rested on the muscles of his shoulders, feeling them flex and ripple with pantherlike grace as he set her on her feet.

"There. That didn't hurt a bit, did it?" The strained quality of Joe's voice brought Mattie abruptly back to reality. She stared disbelievingly at her fingers as they brushed over his shoulders in an unconsciously caressing motion, then snatched them away as if they had been burned. Inside she felt like she was burning, too, and she stepped from his hold, frightened by the sensation.

"No," she agreed blankly, wondering what was happening to her. "That didn't hurt a bit." Except for that fire inside.

There was an awkward, almost waiting silence between them before Mattie turned away, searching blindly for the football.

"Come on," she forced herself to speak. "The sooner we start, the sooner we'll finish."

"Yeah," Joe agreed, his eyes on her back as she walked away. "I'm pretty hungry."

Mattie laughed over her shoulder at him. "You're always hung—"

The look in his eyes stopped her. He was staring at her with a lost and hurt expression, with the look of a man who didn't know whether to fight or flee.

As her eyes met his, however, he blinked, clearing the emotion as effectively as an eraser on a chalkboard. It made Mattie horribly uneasy to witness that phenomenon, because she knew the method well. It was one she had perfected herself at a very early age.

"Joe, are you all right?"

"Sure." Joe looked away.

"You looked . . ."

"Hunger does strange things to me," he interrupted quietly.

They were both silent as they absorbed the implications of that remark.

"How about if we go to my place when we finish here?" Joe asked, breaking the silence with a desperate attempt to put things back on an even keel. "I'll grill hamburgers."

"And hot dogs, too?" Mattie played along, grateful for the escape he offered.

"Hot dogs, too," Joe conceded indulgently. "Come on."

They moved to the center of the field and spent the next thirty minutes with Joe throwing the football and Mattie collecting it. To help sharpen Joe's precision and lessen the amount of area Mattie had to travel in chasing after the football, they devised a system whereby Mattie moved from marker to marker, indicating the spot Joe was to aim. It was no challenge for Joe, of course, with no defensive line to rush him, but he enjoyed being with Mattie. They always enjoyed their time together, no matter how simply spent.

Finally Joe called a halt to the practice.

"My stomach says it's been thirty minutes," he complained.

"Your stomach tells time?" Mattie inquired in assumed awe. "Did you swallow a watch or something? How do you wind it?"

Joe regarded her pityingly. "You must be hungry, too. Your wit is sinking quickly." He grabbed her hand and led her toward the sidelines.

"Wait!" Mattie dug in her heels, and Joe stopped obligingly. "I can't go in the locker room!"

Joe regarded her blankly. "Why not?"

"Why not?" Mattie blustered.

"Yes," Joe repeated slowly, as if he thought she had not understood the question. "Why not?"

"Well . . . there are men in there," Mattie stated flatly.

"I'm sure they've all cleared out by now," Joe pointed out reasonably.

Mattie shook her head. "I'll just wait here."

"Okay," Joe said, shrugging nonchalantly. "But around this time they usually turn on the—"

Suddenly great streams of cold water shot toward them. Mattie studied the cloudless blue sky blankly before realizing that the water was pouring *up* on them instead of down.

"—sprinkler system." Joe finished wryly.

"Eeek!" Mattie shrieked as the cold water began to seep into her jeans. She took a quick step back to get out of range and slipped on the wet grass, ending up at Joe's feet.

Joe couldn't help it. He fell into gales of laughter as he witnessed the stunned look on her face.

Mattie shot him a killing glare, then very deliberately hooked her foot behind his ankle and pushed with all her might on his knee, giving him a mighty shove that brought him to the ground beside her. He sat down rather hard between two thundering sprinkler heads and was promptly drenched.

Now it was Mattie's turn to laugh, and she didn't hold back. Joe watched her, pretending exasperation, but the warm affection buried in his eyes ruined the pose.

Grabbing her wet hands, he hauled her to her feet, studying her between water-spiked lashes. "You are definitely going with me. You need a towel to dry off." His hand still clasping hers, he led her down the tunnel to the locker room.

"You wait here," he instructed. "I'll make sure every-one's gone."

Mattie nodded agreeably, and a moment later he was back, bowing her into the room.

"Behold, my lady. The inner sanctuary of male suprem-acy in the sporting world."

Mattie wrinkled her nose. "The inner sanctuary of male supremacy in the sporting world smells like old gym socks."

Joe looked deeply offended. "That is the smell of vic-tory," he protested grandly. "The sweet, musty smell of success."

"Go take your shower," Mattie advised. "I think some dirt seeped into your brain."

Joe maintained a haughty pose for one more minute, then gave up. "Okay, sweetheart. I'll go scrub my brain. Here—" Joe snared a towel from a nearby stack and threw it to her "—you dry off. I should be out in a second."

Mattie patted her face dry with the towel. "Can I look around while you're in the shower?" Her eyes moved around the room curiously.

"Sure," Joe answered carelessly, pulling the hem of his jersey from his tight uniform pants.

"What's behind that door?" Mattie asked hurriedly, pulling her eyes away from the expanse of tanned skin pre-senting itself.

"Training room." Joe's voice was muffled now as he pulled the jersey over his head.

Mattie scrambled toward the indicated door without looking back. By the time Joe had removed his jersey, her hand was on the knob.

"I'll look around in here while you shower," she told the door, refusing to look at Joe again.

"You forgot your towel," Joe told her chidingly, moving up behind her to drape it around her neck. "I don't want you to get sick, sitting around in those wet clothes."

Mattie took a shallow breath. "I—they'll dry soon, I'm sure. It's rather... warm in here, isn't it?"

Joe studied her rigid profile curiously and didn't answer. Finally, as the silence dragged out, he sighed. "I'll go take my shower."

Mattie went slack with a relief she didn't understand as Joe moved to the showers at the opposite side of the room. A feeling had begun when he lifted her from the stands, as if she were finely balanced on a taut wire and about to go over the edge. It was like nothing she had ever experienced before, and it frightened her to feel that way with Joe. What was happening to her?

The muffled rush of water as Joe turned on the shower broke into her thoughts. The idea of Joe, standing beneath the spray of hot water as he soaped his hard, long body made her suddenly sweaty palm close on the doorknob and twist it to the right. She all but catapulted into the training room and stood there, looking around blindly.

The room rather strongly resembled a chamber of horrors from an old Bela Lugosi movie. There were machines of torture even old Bela hadn't thought of, Mattie observed interestedly, moving farther into the room. It was all black padding, gleaming chrome and weights, making Mattie feel as if she had just stepped into another world. Her idea of exercise was clambering over some rocks to get a shot of a wild horse. No wonder football players got paid so much money, she thought in enlightenment. It was obviously blood money for the pain they went through in rooms like this.

When she heard the rolling sound of water, Mattie moved toward it cautiously. Dodging benches and bar-

bells, she crossed the room. Tucked into a previously unnoticed corner, blocked off by a thin partition, was a tub
full of bubbling water.

And in it was a huge, absolutely naked man.

At first Mattie thought he was dead, so still did he lay.
Frozen to the spot in horror, she whispered, "Oh, my
God."

The prayer was loud enough to bring the dead man's eyes
open. Except that he wasn't dead at all, Mattie realized be-
latedly. He was just resting in the boiling water.

"Well, hi there, honey," the man drawled, studying her
unself-consciously from the tub. "Lookin' for something?"

Mattie, horribly threatened by the sight of this huge man
lounging before her, couldn't speak. Her eyes remained
riveted on his face, steadfastly ignoring the massive chest
and long body thankfully hidden under the rolling water.

"You sure are a pretty little thing," the man continued
blithely, shifting to rise from the tub.

Mattie turned her back with a muffled shriek, listening
as the water sloshed wildly as he rose from the tub.

"Shy, too," the man continued musingly, wrapping a
towel around his hips. Unfortunately, he had big hips and
a small towel and quite a bit of him remained uncovered.
"Still, you can't be too shy, sneaking into the locker room
like this. That's okay, honey," he assured her blithely,
moving to stand in front of Mattie. "I like women who
know what they want. Especially if what they want is me."

When he reached for her, Mattie backed away like a
hunted animal, her eyes wide with shock. The phrase, out
of the frying pan and into the fire, kept chasing through her
mind as she backed away from her pursuer.

"Aw, come on, honey," the man wheedled. "You don't
have to play hard to get with me."

"No, please," Mattie pleaded softly, holding out her arms in front of her as if to ward him off. "I didn't— I wasn't looking for you. I didn't know you were here. Please, let me leave."

The man laughed triumphantly when Mattie came up hard against a wall, halting her retreat. "You found me anyway, angel. Must be your lucky day."

When his hands closed over her shoulders, Mattie screamed as an unreasonable fear overtook her. It wasn't a delicate, feminine sound, but a full-throated, frightened shriek, a nightmare sound.

The man's hands tightened instinctively around her shoulders, his eyes blank with shock. "Now what did you want to go and do that for, lady? I wasn't gonna hurt you."

Whatever else he had been going to say was lost in the sound of the door as it burst open.

Joe came charging into the room, his eyes wild as they searched for Mattie and found her held against the wall by one of his teammates. Mattie's captor had fifty pounds on Joe, but that didn't seem to matter as Joe grabbed his shoulders and pushed him roughly against the wall.

Joe's hair was still wet and tousled, Mattie noticed inconsequentially. He had obviously been in the middle of dressing when he had heard her scream. Although he did have on his jeans, the top button was undone, and his shirt was open completely, revealing a broad chest covered with whirls of dark hair arrowing down to that open button. The shirt clung damply to his skin in places, serving only to emphasize his sheer masculinity. Witnessing the rage in his eyes, Mattie didn't know who she was more frightened of at the moment, Joe or her captor.

"What did you do to her, Jackson?" Joe snarled dangerously, his hands tightening on the other man's arms as he kept him pinned against the wall. "What the hell did you think you were doing?"

Jackson read the wild rage in Joe's eyes and answered in a soothing tone. "Joe, I didn't hurt her. I wasn't trying to hurt her, okay? I was just joking around."

"You frightened her," Joe roared, his face tight with anger and—fear? "You made her scream."

"I didn't mean to scare her," Jackson insisted, not moving, not willing to give Joe an excuse to hit. Bill Jackson wasn't stupid. He didn't tangle with tigers protecting their young, and he didn't fight with a man protecting his woman. "Lady," he pleaded quietly. "Tell him I didn't hurt you."

"He—he didn't hurt me, Joe," Mattie said dutifully, as wary of Joe in this mood as Bill Jackson was. "He really didn't hurt me."

Joe didn't even seem to hear, his eyes focused intently on Jackson. "You had her pinned to the wall when I came in. She sounded terrified when she screamed."

"Joe, I thought she was one of the fans. You know how they sneak in here sometimes. I thought she was looking for a little action...."

"This is my friend. She was waiting for me."

"I understand that now, Joe," Bill told him carefully. "I hung around after the guys left so that I could have the whirlpool to myself. When she came in, I thought—well, you know what I thought. I was just having a little fun."

"Don't *ever* touch Mattie again," Joe warned him dangerously. "Don't ever get near her again."

Bill held his hands up peaceably. "Your lady is safe from me, Joe."

Their eyes held for one more tension-fraught moment before Joe moved slowly away, releasing his teammate.

Mattie let out a deep, relieved breath as the anger faded from Joe's eyes and they seemed to focus once again on her.

"Mattie, are you all right?" His voice was achingly gentle now, and Mattie could only nod.

Bill Jackson moved away, but neither of them noticed as Joe's hands cupped her face. "Are you sure he didn't hurt you?" Joe's voice pleaded for reassurance, and Mattie gave it to him.

"He didn't hurt me. I—I shouldn't have screamed like that."

"He shouldn't have touched you," Joe corrected harshly.

"I think he understands that now," Mattie agreed seriously, her eyes meeting his. Her hands lifted and closed around the bulging muscles of his upper arms. "Thank you for—" She broke off awkwardly, her eyes skittering away from his. "I was so scared . . ."

Joe muttered a muffled curse and pressed her gently against his hard, straining body, offering silent comfort. "You're okay, now, Mattie," he whispered into her hair. "I'd never let anyone hurt you. Never."

Mattie closed her eyes on the words. She believed him. She heard the hard conviction in his voice.

Oh Joe, she wondered in silent despair, where were you ten years ago when I so badly needed that protection? Where were you when I wasn't strong enough to protect myself?

Mattie shuddered delicately at the memory of that time, then sighed, comforted, as Joe tightened his arms around her.

He was with her now. He would always be with her now.

Four

———

Mattie walked reluctantly down a passageway that seemed to stretch forever. Her footsteps echoed hollowly, emphasizing her hesitancy. Joe had said to meet him in the players' lounge, Mattie thought vexedly, but was this the passageway he had shown her before the game or had she fallen down Alice's rabbit hole? Mattie was so preoccupied with looking for the White Rabbit that her first inkling of another presence came when her bent head rammed solidly into a massive, masculine chest.

The force of that blow would have knocked any ordinary man off his feet or at least back a step or two. Mattie herself landed ignominiously on her delicate little backside. The bull elephant in front of her didn't even flinch.

Mattie's stunned eyes focused on cleat-encased feet and rose...and rose...and rose slowly over dirt-smudged white uniform pants, muscular thighs—each easily the size of a baby redwood—a tight waist and a massive chest with the

number 53 spread on the straining jersey. The man's
shoulders stretched forever, Mattie thought with awe. And
that was with no pads beneath the uniform. Then Mattie's
eyes lighted on his face, and she swallowed audibly.

He looked mean. Very mean. The bottom half of his face
was covered with a scruffy stubble, as though he hadn't
shaved in two or three days. His jaw was square and hard.

Mattie swallowed again. "H-hello...*sir.*"

A deep, rusty voice boomed like the wrath of God from
that massive chest. "What are you doing here?"

If it was an accusation, Mattie was ready to admit to any
crime. She was also ready to turn tail and run. She may be
little, but when faced with a male mastodon, she could be
quick. It took another second or two of panicked planning—escape routes to South America and such—before
Mattie's normal good sense reasserted itself. Joe had asked
her to be here, she reminded herself bracingly. If all else
failed, she could run like hell.

With that comforting thought firmly in mind, Mattie
picked herself up delicately, testing gingerly for any broken bones or life-threatening contusions. Not immediately
finding any, she deigned to answer. "I'm looking for Joe
Ryan."

This time the rumble was derisive. "You and half the fe-
male population of Texas."

"No, really," Mattie insisted. "Joe asked me to meet him
here."

"Sure, little girl. *Wives* wait here. Ryan ain't married.
Beat it." Number 53 was brusque. He'd heard it all before.

Mattie was irritated. Fleetingly the realization that she
wasn't having much luck with Joe's teammates ran through
her mind. Before she could consider a wise course of action, she began heatedly, "Listen, Mr....53—"

But Mr. 53 was not listening to the troublesome little lady berating him. His eyes had drifted beyond her, and the hard, mean face and wild eyes softened like chewing gum on a July-hot sidewalk. Mattie's tirade halted abruptly, leaving her open-mouthed in absolute astonishment.

Number 53 brushed past Mattie—Dumbronkowski was the name sewn on the back of the jersey—and met the slight woman coming down the tunnel. She was almost as small as Mattie herself, a pretty redhead with flashing green eyes and a slim build. Slim, that was, except for the fact that she was easily eight months pregnant.

"Jen!" Mattie heard Dumbronkowski roar gently. "What are you doing here? I told you to wait in the stands. I was going to come for you after I took my shower. You shouldn't have come to the game anyway. You'll strain yourself, trying to do so much. You push yourself too hard, beloved." He continued to berate gently as Jen reached up and brushed a kiss across his sweaty, dirt-smudged cheek, replacing his admonishing expression with one of such fatuous adoration that Mattie simply stared.

"Marion, darling, I'm fine," Jen assured him indulgently. "I wanted to tell you how well you played—even though they had you double-teamed."

Dumbronkowski—*Marion*—Mattie corrected herself, began again to fuss over Jen, completely oblivious to Mattie's continued presence.

"Mattie." Joe's voice came from behind her, and Mattie jumped startled.

"Joe!"

Joe regarded her curiously. "Have you been waiting long?"

"No! No," she denied dazedly. "I've just been talking with—Marion." There was still an undertone of faint hysteria in her tone, and Joe's eyes narrowed consideringly.

"Freight's our nose guard," he murmured solemnly.

Mattie studied the straight blade of Joe's nose carefully. "He's doing a very good job."

Joe shook his head, smiling. "Mattie, a nose guard doesn't—"

But Mattie was bubbling with laughter, her eyes gleaming. "Freight? You call him Freight?"

Joe regarded her incredulously. "You don't honestly think any of us are going to call him Marion, do you?"

Both Mattie and Joe turned to study the huge six-foot-five, 265-pound linebacker hovering protectively over the redhead.

"Jen did," Mattie noted.

"Jen is his wife," Joe pointed out dryly.

"Is this their first child?" Mattie asked idly.

"Good Lord, no! This will be their fifth."

"Their fifth!" Mattie was incredulous. "But—but—" She gestured vaguely to the couple. "He's *fussing* so."

Joe regarded her oddly. "He loves her, Mattie."

"He loves her," Mattie repeated blankly, her eyes on the couple. She said nothing more about Marion and Jen Dumbronkowski, but her eyes remained on them as she changed the subject.

"He wasn't going to let me wait for you," she told Joe idly.

"Oh?"

Mattie nodded solemnly. "He thought I was some football floozy out to break your heart."

Joe smiled ruefully. "We all kind of try to protect each other from them."

"Are there many? Football floozies, I mean?" Mattie repeated the words with relish.

Joe answered carefully. "A fair number, I guess."

Mattie looked away. "Do they—do they bother you much?"

Joe shrugged. "Quarterback is a glamour position. They want the thrill of being seen with a football player. They don't want me."

Mattie tentatively reached out and touched his hand, and Joe's questioning eyes flew to hers. "Then they don't know what they're missing."

Joe smiled slowly, a haunting light burned in his eyes. "Damn, you're something."

Mattie drew her hand self-consciously from his and squared her shoulders. "So, onward and upward. Ready to go?"

Mattie and Joe were heading for Joe's cabin in the Hill Country. Joe had told her days ago that he needed to go "winterize" the cabin, and Mattie had eagerly volunteered to help. The Hill Country outside of Austin was one of the most beautiful areas in Texas, and she wanted to see Joe's own little piece of it.

"Don't expect much," Joe warned her lightly. "It's just a weekend escape. Nothing fancy."

"Indoor plumbing?" Mattie questioned hopefully.

Joe laughed. "Indoor plumbing," he agreed. "Let's go."

When they drew even with Jen and Marion Dumbronkowski, Joe stopped. Marion ceased scolding his wife long enough to study Mattie suspiciously.

"Joe!" Jen cried welcomingly, placing a friendly kiss against his cheek. "It's so good to see you. How have you been?"

As Joe and Jen fell into a lively discussion, Mattie's guileless gaze locked with Marion. She read the distrust in his eyes, and a mischievous imp overtook her—fueled, no doubt, by her feeling of safety in Joe's presence.

Wrinkling her nose in an unconsciously enchanting gesture, she surreptitiously stuck out her tongue.

Freight's eyes widened for one incredulous moment, then he burst into a roaring roll of laughter. It's sheer volume startled Mattie.

Joe and Jen broke off their conversation to study the other two with friendly curiosity.

"I guess you know this one, huh, Joe?" Freight's voice rumbled out proddingly.

Joe took the hint. Smiling wryly, he made the introductions. "Sorry. Mattie, I'd like you to meet Jen and Freight Dumbronkowski. Jen, Freight, this is my...friend, Mattie Grey."

Mattie didn't even notice the hesitation, but Freight did, and his eyes sharpened.

"You can call me Marion," Dumbronkowski told her, holding her hand with a delicate awkwardness.

Mattie suddenly realized that the knowledge of his own strength must have been hard learned and she relaxed. After all, he had laughed when she stuck her tongue out at him, hadn't he?

Joe made a strangled sound in his throat at the invitation, and Marion's eyes turned to challenge his fiercely. While they were locked in silent combat, Jen moved closer to Mattie to whisper confidingly, "When he asks you to call him Marion, you know he likes you."

Mattie smiled at her, flattered. "Does that mean he doesn't like Joe?"

"Oh, no!" Jen was vehement. "He never lets any of the guys call him Marion. He says it doesn't convey the proper image." Jen laughed charmingly, and Mattie suddenly knew that, for Jen, the world revolved around her huge, gentle husband.

"Joe tells me you have four children," Mattie murmured. "I take it Marion didn't press you to name any of them Marion, Jr."

Jen looked horrified. "No indeed. Before each baby was born, he spent months trying to sell me on names like Bruiser and Mack."

"And did he?" Mattie inquired interestedly, muffling a giggle as she pictured what a Bruiser Dumbronkowski would look like.

Jen shook her head. "He caved in after each of our girls was born. Not a Bruiser in the lot."

"Each of your girls?" Mattie repeated incredulously. "You have *four* girls?"

The redhead laughed delightedly at Mattie's expression and patted her bulging abdomen. "Maybe five."

It was Mattie's turn to shake her head. "Is he going to make you keep trying until you get a boy?" she asked seriously.

Jen regarded her oddly. "Not at all. He adores our girls. They smile and Marion melts. It's just that we both love children. And our children are a very powerful affirmation of our love for each other."

"Aren't you—worried about giving him all those daughters?" Mattie questioned Jen with helpless fear.

Joe's voice broke in before Jen could give voice to the questions in her eyes. "We should be hitting the road, Mattie."

Mattie nodded a little vaguely and murmured goodbye to the Dumbronkowskis. They had taken perhaps five steps down the tunnel when Marion's booming voice stopped their progress.

"You bring your friend to dinner next week, Joe."

Joe turned to meet Marion's understanding gaze.

"You're on," he called back. His eyes shifted to Mattie. "Okay?"

Mattie smiled. "Okay." She took one more look at the seemingly mismatched couple before them—Jen so slight and Marion so threatening—and walked away with a thoughtful expression.

"Joe, what do you think ... love is?"

Joe stilled, the ax he was using to chop logs halting in midair, as Mattie's hesitant question reached him. She was supposed to be helping him stack wood for the winter months, but she had been staring into space for well over five minutes. Now he knew why.

He brought the tool down carefully, his breath misting in the frigid air. It was a damn cold day, he thought irrelevantly. "What kind of love, Mattie?"

Mattie faced him, puzzled. "You know ... *love*."

"The kind of love between a man and a woman," Joe defined factually.

"Yes."

"That's a tough one," Joe told her wryly. "I think—I've always thought—that love like that is gentle, but not always. Protective, but not smothering. Love is not feeling...complete without her beside you. And a smile means more than all the words in the world. There's a warmth where there used to be an emptiness—" He broke off in disgust, running his hands through his wind-tousled black hair. "This sounds so trite."

"No!" Mattie protested, self-consciously blinking away the tears in her eyes. "No. It sounds ... beautiful. I didn't know men thought like that. But that's not all there is to—loving, is there?"

"What makes you say that?" Joe was wary.

"Well," Mattie began reasonably, "what you described is the way I feel about you."

Joe took a deep breath, his eyes intent on hers. "Is it, Mattie?" His voice was muffled.

"Yes. Especially the part about feeling warm when you're around and not empty anymore. But there's *more*."

"Yes," Joe admitted softly. "There's more. Between a couple in love, there's also a ... need to physically express that love," Joe explained carefully, his eyes shifting away awkwardly.

"Sex," Mattie defined flatly.

Joe turned back to challenge her. "Making love."

"Is there a difference?"

"Oh, yes, there's a difference. Mattie, sex can mean nothing, or it can be only physically satisfying. Making love can touch the soul." Joe paused a second or two before adding, "I think."

Mattie peeked up at him. "You think?" she repeated politely.

Joe shrugged wryly. "I'm probably not the man to ask about it. I've had sex, Mattie. I've never made love."

Mattie shifted uncomfortably as the conversational person changed from "a man" and "a woman" to Joe himself, but she didn't want to relinquish the subject yet. Too many questions were unanswered after her introduction to Jen and Marion Dumbronkowski.

"Not all men feel that way, surely," she persisted nervously. "I mean, do you suppose every time Marion makes love to his wife, he sits up and thinks, 'Gee, that really touched my soul'?"

Joe's mouth twitched irrepressibly. "No," he agreed solemnly.

"Aha!"

"I think sometimes he just *lies* there and thinks, 'Gee, that really touched my soul'!"

Joe's twinkling eyes met Mattie's, inviting her to share the laughter. Mattie could not resist. Together their mirth rose on the crisp air and danced on the wind.

Finally, when the laughter had subsided, they resumed their task of storing wood in the shed. They worked in silent harmony for a while before Joe broke the silence.

"Why all the sudden curiosity about love, Mattie?" He kept his voice painstakingly casual, but his body was tense.

Mattie shrugged self-consciously. "I guess it was seeing Jen and Marion," she admitted uneasily. "He's so much bigger than she is, but so gentle. I—I didn't know it could be like that."

Joe watched her closely. "Freight would walk through the fires of hell rather than hurt Jen or his girls."

"But what if he got mad at her?" Mattie persisted. "What if he got really mad at her?"

Joe realized that they were no longer discussing Freight and Jen. There was so much more in Mattie's voice, fear and confusion. He knew his answer would be very, very important to the future of their relationship, and he struggled for the right words.

"If he got very angry with her I imagine, knowing Freight, that he would punch a wall."

"He might hit her," Mattie said in a distant little voice. "She's smaller than he is."

"Mattie—" Joe shook his head "—Jen could flatten Freight with one look. He lives for her. He adores her."

"But physically—"

"No man would ever raise a hand to the woman he loves," Joe declared with flat finality. "No real man. Oh, there are some pretty sorry specimens masquerading as men, but they're not. Only cowards hurt those weaker than themselves. Only cowards intentionally hurt others at all. A man doesn't prove he's a man by how much pain he can inflict, Mattie. He proves it by how much love he can give.''

Mattie's stunned eyes locked on his face.

"Don't you see, sweetheart?" Joe asked softly. "Freight may have the muscles, but he's given Jen the power. There are many kinds of strengths. Love is the biggest of them all.''

"The ultimate weapon," Mattie muttered cynically.

"The ultimate healer," Joe corrected her quietly, pain glimmering in his eyes. "The ultimate healer, Mattie.''

Later, after the wood had been chopped and stored, the cabin cleaned from top to bottom and a long, rambling walk in the surrounding woods taken, they were both seated comfortably on the floor in front of the fireplace. Mattie was leaning against the overstuffed couch, and Joe, lying full length on the floor, had a cup of hot chocolate balanced on his flat stomach. The silence was broken only by the crackling of the fire, and their occasional sleepy attempts at conversation. They both knew that they had to leave for Dallas soon, but for now, neither was capable of moving.

It felt right, Mattie mused silently. Being here with Joe, warm and sheltered from the biting wind outside, comfortable with the silence and with the words. He was so warm and relaxing....

"Like a cup of cocoa," she murmured, unconsciously happy.

Joe roused himself sufficiently to question her words. "You want some of my hot cocoa?"

Mattie smiled, realizing that she had spoken aloud. "No, I was just thinking out loud. I'm so comfortable here with you. You're like a cup of cocoa on a cold day.''

Joe was silent for a moment, his eyes closed. "Thanks," he finally muttered dryly. "I think."

Mattie gathered all of her strength and turned her head slightly. "Well, it was a compliment! You're my best friend, Joe." The last came out in a quiet, solemn tone. Saying it aloud somehow made it a commitment in Mattie's mind, and it was a commitment she did not take lightly.

Joe took a deep breath, his eyes fixed on the ceiling. "Mattie, I don't want..."

But whatever he had been going to say was lost in the unmistakable sounds of sleet and ice beating against the windows and roof of the cabin. Joe surged to his feet, placing the almost empty cup on a nearby table and crossed to the door. He twisted the knob impatiently and threw the door open.

A freezing rush of air ran in, like a thief from the night, and Mattie shivered reflexively. Sleet was raining down, mixed liberally with drops of pure ice. The late afternoon sky had darkened to a nighttime shade.

"Good Lord," Joe breathed in amazement. "It's snowing, too."

"Snowing!" Mattie jumped to her feet and joined him in the doorway. "It can't be snowing. This is Texas!"

"Nevertheless," Joe began, turning to her with a little-boy grin. But his amusement died instantly when he met her gaze. He became dazed, as though he had just been punched in the stomach with a sledgehammer. "Mattie...oh God, we have to get out of here!" He dragged one hand through his thick hair. "Mattie, gather your things. We have to leave before this gets any worse. These roads are bad enough in the summer..." The last statement was tossed over his shoulder as he slammed the door and strode to the hearth to bank the fire. He was clearly agitated and tense, Mattie realized curiously. She crossed the room and plunked herself firmly on the couch.

"Mattie," Joe said impatiently, spying her on the couch. "We have to hurry!"

Mattie shook her head deliberately, her chin rising stubbornly. "If you think that I—" she pointed to herself "—am going driving on those treacherous hill-country backroads with you—" she pointed to him "—when it's doing this—" she waved her hand expansively to encompass the great outdoors "—then you are insane."

Joe held back reluctant laughter and dropped beside her on the couch. "Mattie, you are so . . . don't you realize that if this keeps up, these roads are going to be impassable? There's no telling how long we'll be stranded here."

"Well, we have plenty of food, don't we?" Mattie pointed out reasonably.

"Yes, but—"

"And heaven knows we have enough firewood to last us into the next century."

"That's not the point." Joe tried again.

But Mattie reached for the radio and turned it on, drowning out Joe's words with the determinedly cheerful voice of a local DJ.

"—tional Weather Service had issued a traveler's advisory for Austin and the surrounding Hill Country through 6:00 p.m. tomorrow evening. Most roads in the Hill Country are already impassable, and city streets are rapidly worsening. The sleet and freezing rain are expected to continue for at least another hour, with accumulations of up to two inches in the city and four inches in parts of the Hill Country—" Joe's eyes met Mattie's in silent defeat. "—possibly turning to snow with expected accumulations—are you ready for this, y'all?—of up to four inches by morning. With no equipment to handle the ice and snow, Austin is going to be a winter wonderland by morning, folks. So build a fire, grab your loved one and practice some serious heat conservation.''

"Stranded," Joe muttered blankly. "For days...Mattie." His eyes met hers intently. "I didn't know this was going to happen. I never thought—"

Mattie studied him with unveiled amazement. "Of course you didn't," she reassured him soothingly, snapping off the radio. "Why would you want to be trapped up here with me?"

"Now there's a question," Joe agreed mockingly beneath his breath.

"What?"

Joe swallowed audibly and shook his head. "Nothing...nothing."

Mattie shrugged. "Okay. We'd better get organized here. We'll need to bring in some more wood and open the faucets a bit and keep that fire going. Do you have any kerosene lamps, just in case?"

Joe's eyes were bemused. "Mattie, I don't think—"

"You don't have the kerosene lamps? That's okay," she told him forgivingly. "I know you have a flashlight in the car. But you really ought to have some alternate form of lighting here. You never know—"

"Mattie," Joe broke in desperately. "I *do* have kerosene lamps."

"Why did you say you didn't, then?"

"I didn't say I didn't! Why would I say I didn't when I did if I didn't—" Joe broke off abruptly. "Forget it, Mattie. Just forget it. I don't know what I said. You...you *confuse* me so much!"

"But—"

"No! Not another word. I'm going to get some wood."

Joe turned and strode out the back door. Mattie shook her head sadly. "Poor man. That cocoa went straight to his head."

Joe stood in the dark, cold woodshed and let loose a stream of imaginative and heartfelt curses. Snowbound, for who knew how long, alone with Mattie. And she was treating it like an outing with the Girl Scouts. She hadn't one thought of what he would go through trying to keep his hands off her. Oh, no! Not one smidgen of an idea that he might try to take advantage of the situation. No, her innocent mind was taken up with the adventure of it all.

While his own brain, Joe acknowledged disgustedly, wasn't doing much of anything but laughing as his body reacted.

"Damn."

Her best friend. Mattie had said that he was her best friend, Joe remembered, his face etched with a curious gentleness. A part of him wanted to rant and rave and demand much more than friendship, to say that he would have everything from her or nothing at all. But for the most part he felt a swelling joy and gratitude to know that she felt *something* for him. Friendship was something real, Joe thought determinedly. Something he could build on and strengthen, and...snowbound for days...alone with Mattie.

"Damn," he repeated.

Okay guys, he silently addressed the various troublesome parts of his mind and body, let's be rational about this. So you're going to be alone with her. Big deal. You've been alone with her before.

Not really, his body jeered in response. Not completely alone, thrown together all night long, with nothing to stop you from taking what you really want, really need.

Mattie and I will find things to do, Joe told himself sternly. There won't be time to think about what I want.

Things to do? his body taunted. Oh, yeah. Sitting in front of the fire with your arm around her, her head resting on your chest. Snuggling up to each other to keep warm....

Things that don't require touching, Joe amended tautly, his mind full of vivid images of touching Mattie, holding Mattie, loving Mattie....

You think you can stop yourself from touching her?

I'm strong. I can handle it.

The disbelieving and contemptuous silence of his mind spoke for itself.

Joe began to methodically pile logs in the canvas carry-all he kept in the shed. Despite the dictates of his body, he knew that he would not try to force any intimacy on Mattie. Not when he wanted so much more. The loving without the love would be a bitter pill to swallow, and it was not a medicine that Joe was willing to take. Not while there was a chance of having it all. The friendship she offered was such a big part of the whole, he thought achingly. Affection, and better yet, trust were such an implicit part of that friendship. And given a choice, Joe acknowledged, he would take her friendship with a promise of forever over one night of possessing her body.

I must be a masochist, he decided grimly as he left the woodshed and moved toward the cabin through the snow.

Evening came quickly and silently, finding them in the same positions in front of the fireplace as before. Mattie wore an old T-shirt of Joe's that he had found and her faded blue jeans. It reached well past midthigh, and Mattie thought that it would make very comfortable nightware once she removed her jeans.

She tried to relax, but she was picking up an indefinable tension from Joe. He had been this way ever since the freezing rain had started. Maybe he just needed to talk, Mattie thought reasonably.

"Talk to me," she ordered.

Joe, jolted out of his confused thoughts, turned to face her warily. "What about?"

"Anything," Mattie insisted vaguely. "Ships and shoes and sealing wax—"

"—and cabbages and kings—"

"—and why the sea is boiling hot—"

"—and whether pigs have wings." They both broke off, laughing, and Mattie brightened.

"I've always loved that poem," she told him happily.

Joe nodded. "Me, too. I used to beg my mother to read it to me every night for three years. Finally, she got sick of it and made me memorize the whole thing."

Mattie studied him thoughtfully. "What was your mother like?"

Joe's face softened with loving memories. "She was a wonderful lady. Very warm and gracious. A little shy around strangers. She adored my father, and he would have laid down and made a rug of himself if she had said the word."

Mattie listened to his words, but they seemed unreal to her, pure fiction. Joe's father must have been a strong, proud man to have raised Joe as he was. She couldn't picture him bowing to the wishes of a weaker being, even his wife . . . especially his wife.

"They're both gone now?" Mattie asked hesitantly, then wanted to call the words back as she witnessed the flash of pain in Joe's eyes.

"They died in a light plane crash. They were flying back to the ranch when the plane went down." There was a wealth of sad regret in his words.

"Ranch?" Mattie picked up on that to distract him. "The ranch you told me you grew up on? Where's it at?"

Joe smiled at her oddly. "Where it's always been. Waiting for me to come back."

"You still own it?" Mattie was surprised.

"All my life I've intended to be a rancher, sweetheart. It's what I grew up with, it's what I love. I even took my college degree in land management."

"But you're a football player," Mattie pointed out irrefutably.

"Football has always been just a game to me. I played in college for the fun of it. I never intended to go pro."

"But after your parents died..." Mattie filled in understandingly.

Joe shrugged a little awkwardly. "I sort of lost direction after that," he admitted softly, gripping her hand gently. "I couldn't go back there. The memories...all of our plans were still so much a part of the place, of me. We had planned to work the land together, to build together."

Mattie watched his sadness and felt sad. "So you decided to play football instead."

Joe nodded. "I turned pro right after graduation, but I never intended to abandon the ranch. I always knew that someday, I'd go back to it."

"And it's someday?"

Joe smiled at her understanding. "I'm ready to go home. I need to go home. This will be my last season. I'm retiring to raise cattle and wildflowers."

"Retiring?" Mattie scoffed lightly. "You're only thirty-two."

"I'm an old man by football standards, Mattie. I want to be young again. I want to start building things."

Mattie raised her head questioningly, and Joe carefully dammed the emotion in his eyes. "What kind of things?"

He shifted uneasily. Love, he answered silently. A family, a life. But he knew he could not say the words aloud. Not now, not yet. "Come on, sweetheart," he said, changing the subject. "It's getting late. Get ready for bed." He gave her a gentle shove toward the cabin's one and only bedroom, with its narrow single bed.

Mattie resisted. "Where will you sleep?"

"Right here in front of the fire," Joe indicated the floor easily. "I'll be warm enough."

Mattie nodded doubtfully and turned back toward the bedroom. "Joe..."

He turned to meet her eyes.

"I really like your cabin. Thank you for bringing me."

"Thank you for coming," he responded quietly.

"I—I'd like to see your ranch sometime," she said tentatively.

Joe turned away carefully. This was the opening he had been waiting for. "Christmas is coming up," he told her with every bit of casualness he could muster. "We could spend it there, together."

Mattie's heart leaped. "Wouldn't you rather spend Christmas with somebody else?" she asked awkwardly, shifting from one foot to the other on the cold wood floor.

Joe turned to face her, his eyes solemn. "Mattie, you're my best friend. Who else would I spend Christmas with?"

"But before we met—"

"Before we met I spent the holidays with my neighbor at the ranch, Cole Baron."

"Won't he miss you this year?"

Joe shook his head, a quiet smile deep in his eyes. "I doubt if Cole will even remember my name this Christmas. This is going to be his first with his new wife."

"Oh."

"How about if we stop at their house on the way to the ranch? That would give us a chance to exchange presents without intruding."

Mattie stared at him without answering, and Joe saw a kind of suppressed yearning in her eyes.

"Mattie—"

"It's just that I'm not much good at Christmas stuff," she burst out in self-defense, wrapping her arms around her body to ward off a sudden chill. "I haven't had much practice at it, you see."

Joe narrowed his eyes on a wave of pain. Sometimes she unconsciously let these clues about her childhood drop, and Joe was forming a grim and empty picture of what it must have been like for her. She never spoke of those years, never mentioned her parents or any family. Joe thought that she must have never known love, or warmth, or caring. Maybe that explained why she didn't recognize what lay in his eyes.

"I'll take my chances," he told her huskily. "Okay?"

Mattie met his eyes helplessly, wanting so badly to accept that it was almost a physical pain within her. "Okay."

"Good. Now go to sleep, Mattie. You're going to need all of your strength to shovel us out of here tomorrow."

"*I'm* going to shovel us out of here tomorrow?" she demanded incredulously. "And what, pray tell, are *you* going to be doing?"

Joe grinned wickedly. "Supervising."

Mattie threw a pillow at him and ran for cover.

Joe caught the pillow in one large hand and watched her run. Away. Again.

* * *

No more than three hours later Mattie woke up shivering so hard that her bones ached. She was curled up into a ball, with a down comforter swathing her from her neck to her toes, and she was still so cold she couldn't even feel her face. With a muffled sigh, she pulled herself from the bed, clutching the blanket around her slender form. She crossed to the old-fashioned radiator in the corner and touched it. Cold, stone cold. Sometime in the past three hours the heat had gone out. Mattie had a feeling that a lot of power lines had snapped under the weight of ice coating them, and that they weren't the only ones without power. On the other hand, there was a roaring fire in the very next room. Joe would have to share.

Hiking the comforter up to her calves, Mattie stumbled to the living room, her eyes only half-open.

Standing above Joe's peacefully slumbering form, she sighed. "Joe."

No response. Not even a twitch.

Shuddering as another chill racked her body, Mattie prodded him with her freezing toes. A little more forcefully than was strictly necessary. "Joe!"

"What!" Joe was on his feet before Mattie could so much as blink. His eyes were wild and his hair tousled. "Mattie, what the...?"

Mattie smiled sweetly. "The heat's gone out. I'm freezing my little tootsies off." She promptly plopped down on Joe's blanket and stuck her feet toward the warmth of the fire.

Joe regarded her closely through sleepy eyes. "Your tootsies really aren't that little," he pointed out honestly. "In fact, for someone your size, they're absolutely huge— Ouch—" He broke off with a screech as Mattie slapped her absolutely huge, totally frozen feet against his hairy calf.

"You were saying?" she demanded sweetly. "Absolutely—"

"Gorgeous," Joe substituted hurriedly, moving out of range. "Absolutely gorgeous tootsies. Tootsies men would die for, tootsies that could start a revolution, launch a thousand ships."

"Oh, Joe, I'm too tired to laugh. Don't make me."

Joe rubbed his hands together bracingly, shivering in the cold air. "Look, I'll try to get the heat going again."

"I think the lines have snapped," Mattie told him disinterestedly, luxuriating in the heat of the fire as it bathed her body. "Couldn't we both just sleep here?"

Joe regarded her with deep consternation. "Mattie—"

"You take that side, and I'll take this one," Mattie was being reasonable again, arranging their blankets side by side on the floor with a respectable distance between them.

Joe regarded her helplessly, listening as every one of his good resolutions, so painfully made in the woodshed earlier that day, began to crumble at his feet like a condemned building.

"Look, you can sleep here and I'll sleep in the bedroom—" he tried hopelessly.

"Don't be silly," Mattie told him briskly, already settling in before the fire. "We wouldn't be able to defrost you until August. Go to sleep."

And with that Mattie snuggled deeper into her blanket, sighed once and blissfully drifted off to dreamland.

Joe studied her disbelievingly. Asleep. Here. Half on his blanket. Closing his eyes, he repeated his good intentions to himself, his lips moving silently as he recited them under his breath. After ten minutes he felt marginally stronger and opened his eyes.

Mattie innocently wriggled under the blanket, sighed, and Joe closed his eyes, repeating his silent resolutions all over again.

Five

It was two-thirty in the morning when Joe finally gave up the fight. And only then, he assured himself virtuously, because, in her sleep, Mattie had pressed close to his hard body, cuddling for warmth. Joe stifled a groan as her head made an inviting, nestling motion at his throat and her hips brushed against his own in soft allure.

Dear Lord! How was he supposed to calmly go to sleep when he ached for her from his teeth to his toes? Just to touch her one time would be enough.

The nagging voice in his mind, which had made him repeat his good intentions six times before lying down beside her must have done the sensible thing and dozed off hours ago, for it did not taunt his rationalizations again. He could touch her now, he thought, unconsciously clenching his fists. The softness of her skin, the warmth of her body. It would be enough just to touch; he wouldn't need more.

Even as he heard the words in his head, he knew he was lying to himself. He would always need more. But he also knew that he couldn't stop himself now.

As though watching from a distance, a disinterested observer, he saw his hand lift slowly to brush a dark sweep of curls from her forehead. A silent, graceful motion that spoke evocatively of his need for her. The second his skin made contact with hers, though, all illusion of distance was erased. It was as if a white-hot flame had been turned on inside of him. His breath caught somewhere deep in his chest, his heart raced and his eyes closed in an agony of pleasure.

Mattie, deeply asleep and innocently unaware, snuggled closer.

Joe swallowed thickly and allowed his fingers to drift down the sweet curve of her soft cheek to her determined chin. Soft, so soft. He leaned down to test that softness with his lips, brushing a butterfly kiss into the dimple he found there. The exploration went on. From her delicate neck to her slender shoulders Joe drew a line with his fingers. The hollow at the base of her throat beckoned his lips, and Joe could not resist, beginning to lose himself in her.

Mattie slowly drifted towards consciousness, vaguely aware of butterflies dancing over her skin. Butterflies...in December... Mattie yanked to complete wakefulness as a hard, male hand moved caressingly over the swell of her breasts. Dear God, not again! Not the nightmare again...

With a strangled little moan, she tore herself away from those hands, blinded by fear and memories as she dragged herself across the cold floor, searching for a place to hide. Tears cascaded down her face silently, endlessly, but she did not sob because she had learned her lesson well. Noise only brought the promise of more pain.

"Mattie!" Joe cried out, feeling something rip inside of him as he watched her drag herself across the floor away from his touch. "Oh God, Mattie..."

Mattie was trembling so badly that she barely heard him. She felt lost in the past. She searched madly for the walls within herself, the walls she could erect to hide behind and that would keep her safe from those hands.

"Mattie, sweetheart, it's Joe." The voice came from a long way away, urgent and tormented and strained. "Do you hear me? It's Joe, just Joe. It was me touching you, only me. Do you understand me, Mattie? It was me. I won't hurt you. I would never hurt you..."

The soothing litany continued until Mattie began to listen, and Joe's voice was hoarse and broken.

"Just Joe. Only touching you. Oh, God, come back to me...sweetheart...."

"Joe?" Mattie's voice was weak, as her eyes finally began to focus on the present again.

Joe drew a deep, shaky breath and rocked back on his heels. "Oh Lord, you scared me there, sweetheart. Don't do that to me again."

Mattie didn't even hear the fear in his shaky plea.

"You were touching me." The words were flat as Mattie's eyes were drawn blindly to the fire. She concentrated on the soft hush of the flames as they lapped against the wood and tried to block out Joe's unsteady breathing behind her.

"I would never hurt you, Mattie," Joe repeated hollowly, rubbing his eyes. "I wasn't trying to hurt you."

Mattie wrapped her arms tightly around her updrawn knees and began to rock her body protectively.

Mattie nodded her head wearily, acknowledging the truth of what he said. "I—I'm sorry I...panicked. I don't know why."

"Don't you?"

Mattie's eyes raced to his as she recognized the gentle dissent in his rough tone. Dear God, what did he know?

"Joe—"

But Joe did not let her finish whatever denial or diversion she was attempting.

"You know, Mattie, ever since we met, I've had this nagging feeling of...recognition. I could never quite figure out what it was, but I know now. It's not your face, or your smile, or the way you walk. It's your eyes, the expression you try to hide in them. The fear, the pain, the wariness. That's what I've seen before." Joe exhaled carefully. "In Janie's eyes."

Mattie flinched as if he had slapped her with the words, and her stiff face whitened in the firelight. Joe's own eyes closed in mute agony.

It was true, he accepted with a silent, overwhelming pain. His beautiful, proud Mattie... The hurt that raced through him was almost paralyzing in its intensity. No rage, not yet. Only the unbearable knowledge of what she had suffered, and he allowed that pain to consume him totally. Now he understood the fear of physical closeness, the wary evasions, the silent terror. The knowledge had been building within him for a long time, but seeing her dragging herself across the floor, trying to hide from him exactly as Janie had done...

Mattie slumped in defeat, her forehead falling to rest on her drawn-up knees as the memories overtook her and the silence lengthened. A fine trembling that had nothing to do with cold shook her. She would have to tell him now. He had a right to know who and what he had befriended. And now she would lose him, too.

Joe watched her tremble and ached to touch her, to drive the fear away, but he knew that he could not, knew finally

how much a part of her it was. His throat tightened painfully as he watched her head rise slowly, her eyes wide and
glittering with tears she refused to let fall.

When she spoke, her voice was soft and rusty with pain.
"My parents deserted me when I was three. They were
young...they divorced." Her mouth twisted, but it was not
a smile. "They 'loved' me too much to drag me down with
them, I was told. But not enough to give me up for adop-
tion." This was obviously a pain she had dealt with and
accepted long ago. "I grew up in foster homes. No one kept
me for long—just long enough to do their duty by me. Oh
yes, they all did their duty—and collected their money.
Until I was eleven...twelve...thirteen..." Her voice drifted
off, her eyes hard and impenetrable.

A part of Joe wanted to scream at her to stop, not to
torture herself this way, but the best part of him knew that
they both had to hear the words if they would ever be free
of the past. His hands clenched into fists and a muscle
kicked to life in his jaw as she continued in that quiet, curiously emotionless tone.

"When I was eleven, they placed me in a new home. A
man and his wife. She was very sick, I think. She hardly
ever spoke. It was like she was...waiting to die. I was only
eleven—it took me a while to understand that it was because of *him*. It was all because of him. He was very big...
He used to t-touch me...." Mattie stuttered badly, her
throat tight and aching. "He h-hurt me...."

Joe's soft moan was that of an animal in pain, but Mattie was deaf to the sound, blind to him, lost in the past.

"I ran away, but they always took me back...to him.
And he always punished me." Silence. A horrible yawn-
ing, *remembering* silence, and something inside of Joe
ached for the child she had been. "She died when I was
thirteen. They took me away then." Her eyes were blank,

empty. "But I think they forgot a part of me. I think there was something he took that they couldn't get back.... I've never been whole since then."

The tears had slipped from her smoky eyes now, silent and warm as they drifted down her hollow cheeks. No sobs shook her, no cries escaped, but the tears spoke of such deep pain that Joe winced.

His own eyes were burning with tears for the child who had been so abused. There was no doubt in his mind what she was trying to tell him. He understood exactly what it was she had talked so carefully about. Mattie had been sexually and emotionally molested at the ages of eleven...twelve...thirteen. His gallant Mattie had suffered more pain and degradation than any person should ever have to bear. His beautiful, brave Mattie had been left with nightmares and scars across her soul that might never heal.

"He used to call me Matilda. That's why I hate the name so much." His voice echoed in her head and she whimpered in pain. "Hold still, Matilda. You'll love this, Matilda. I love you, Matilda."

Joe's control broke and rage overtook him. It burned in him to the same fiery depths his pain had carved. His body shook with it, his voice trembled with it.

"Why didn't you tell anyone?"

Mattie heard the despairing question, but it did not seem to touch her. Joe's hands closed gently over her upper arms, forcing her limp, pliant body to respond to him.

"Why didn't you tell anyone?" he demanded again, his face twisted with pain.

Mattie answered lifelessly, obscurely. "All those years I spent alone, without a family...I used to dream that someday, somebody would love me."

Joe immediately understood what that bleak little voice was telling him. "No. Oh, no, Mattie. That wasn't love." He shook her urgently, emphasizing what he said. "Mattie, that wasn't love."

"He said it was," Mattie told him stonily, not meeting his eyes. "He said he loved me."

"No, Mattie. He was sick. He hurt you. Love doesn't hurt like that. We talked about it, remember? A man would never hurt the woman he loves. Remember?"

"I remember."

"And he hurt you," Joe persisted grimly.

"Y-yes."

"So he didn't love you," Joe insisted intently.

"He said he did. He said that's why he t-touched me. That touching was the price I had to pay for being...loved."

"Dammit, get it through your head that love is not like that!" Joe's tone was hard and driven, and Mattie seemed to shrink into herself.

"You're angry," she said flatly.

"Hell, yes, I'm angry!" Joe exploded in pain and frustration, his eyes fierce.

Mattie wretched herself from his hold, her face crumbling. "It wasn't my fault," she cried pitifully as the sobs finally came, racking her slender body with a force that frightened Joe. "It wasn't my fault. I didn't want him to...I hated him!"

"Mattie! Oh, Mattie," Joe whispered brokenly, afraid to reach for her. "I know it wasn't your fault. I know. You were a child, an innocent child. Oh God, Mattie, let me hold you," he begged helplessly, his eyes burning. "Please let me hold you...."

Joe knew what he was asking of her. More important, Mattie knew that he was asking her to put aside the nightmare of what that man had done and turn to another man for comfort, which was a frightening move. She had lived alone with the memories for so long they had become a part of her. Now Joe was asking her to share that part of her with him. Joe, she thought achingly. Her best friend, Joe. She didn't hesitate, throwing herself into his pleading arms and burying her tear-stained face against his throat.

"Thank God," Joe whispered tightly, pressing a gentle, soothing kiss to Mattie's temple. "Mattie, cry...let the tears heal you. I'm here to hold you, to keep you safe. I'll always be here for you."

Mattie barely heard the soothing words or felt the desperate, consoling kisses he pressed to her burning face. She only knew that finally she had shared the pain and she could feel the poison seeping from the wound. She would always bear the scars, but maybe now, because of Joe, she could begin to heal.

They stayed like that for a long time, clinging tightly to each other as the dawn began to break on the horizon. Sometimes they spoke, and sometimes they were silent. But even in the silence, an almost tangible wave of communication flowed between them.

"You were touching me," Mattie's voice was husky with confusion as it rose from his shoulder where her face was buried.

Joe smoothed a careful hand over her short dark hair and searched for a defense to the accusation in those four simple words. He could hardly tell her about the need, the hunger, the love he felt, when in Mattie's mind those words, those emotions were only a prelude to violation. He could hardly claim friendship, when she must have felt his body trembling with the uncontrolled desire he felt with her in his arms.

"I didn't mean to frighten you," he finally evaded quietly.

"There—there's not a price for friendship, too, is there, Joe?" Mattie's uncertain and frightened tone clawed into Joe's heart like razor sharp talons.

"No." He swallowed tightly and pressed his lips into her wavy tresses. "No price for friendship."

Mattie sighed and drifted to the edges of sleep.

Joe tightened his hold and stared into the darkness for a long, long time.

When Joe awoke a few hours later, Mattie was still in his arms. Her quiet, shallow breaths brushed against the warm cord of his throat like the most evocative caress, and her head nestled trustingly against his shoulder. He shifted carefully to study her sleeping form.

She was so pretty! She looked so fragile asleep and vulnerable in his arms. But now he knew that there was nothing fragile about Mattie Grey. Something hurt and lost and sad, but never fragile or insubstantial. She had survived a nightmare and somehow found an inner strength to carry her through the memories. Maybe she had lost a part of herself, as she had told him so desparingly last night. He wondered if she understood that she had found something, too.

Easing carefully out of the chair, Joe left Mattie still sleeping. They had spent all of the night holding each other, talking and giving comfort, but he didn't want her to be frightened, waking up in a man's arms.

He stumbled to the kitchen, wryly rubbing the morning stubble on his face. He probably looked like a renegade pirate. Mattie would have run screaming out the door, waking up to him. After putting some coffee on to brew, Joe crossed to the back door to check on the weather.

The freezing rain had stopped, he noted with relief, and the sun was out. The silver drops of melting ice were proof that the thaw had set in. They should be able to leave today.

"Good morning."

Joe drew a steadying breath and turned to face Mattie.

"Good morning."

She looked tired, he thought in concern. Tired and pale. And seemed more than a little uncertain as she hovered awkwardly in the doorway.

"I made some coffee." He crossed to the counter to pour two cups.

"Oh, no."

Joe turned to face Mattie, wounded. "What's wrong with my coffee?"

Mattie answered weakly but good-humoredly. "Other than the fact that it could be used to pave a driveway?"

"Just because your coffee wouldn't kill a petunia—" Joe began defensively.

"It's a good thing, then, isn't it," she said sweetly, "that I've never had a desire to kill a petunia with my coffee?"

Joe snorted and shoved the cup into her hand. "Drink it. You look tired."

The cup halted midway to her lips at his abrupt comment.

"I slept in a chair all night," she reminded him gently.

With me, Joe added silently. "How do you feel?"

Mattie did not pretend to misunderstand. "Funny. A little ... scared."

"Scared?" Joe picked up on that immediately. "Why scared?"

Mattie shrugged uneasily. "You, you know things about me no one else does. It might ..."

"It might what?" Joe prompted, setting his cup on the counter to cross to her side. He cupped her face and forced her to meet his eyes, forced her to remember the hours spent talking in his arms. "It might what, Mattie?"

"Change the way you feel about me." Mattie told him in a rush, her gaze sliding from his gaze.

"Why?"

"You know why," she insisted harshly. "Because I've been—*used*."

"*Used?*" Joe repeated tightly, eyes flaming. "What, like a car?"

"No!" Mattie tried to draw away from the fire in his eyes, but Joe's thumbs forced her chin up.

"Mattie, you're a person. A beautiful lady who has been hurt in a way you should never have had to bear. *It wasn't your fault.* You told me that, and it's the truth. You are not any less a person because of what he did to you. Not to me."

"Do you really believe that?" There was something so hurt and desperate in her shadowed eyes that Joe couldn't answer for a moment.

"I really believe that," he confirmed gently. "What's important is that you believe it."

Mattie searched his eyes. "He never…he only…touched me. He never raped me," she finally managed to say in an embarrassed rush.

Joe wrapped her carefully in his arms, barely breathing until he felt her relax against him. More than anything else he wanted to hold her and show her gentleness, show her what a man could give a woman.

There were all kinds of violation, Joe thought grimly. And Mattie's heart had been violated. That bastard had not raped her body, but he had raped her mind. The scar was just as deep and just as painful.

"I'm glad, sweetheart," he whispered into her tumbled hair. "I'm glad. But it really would not change what I feel for you. Believe that."

Mattie pulled away, surreptitiously brushing a lone tear from her cheek. "Why do you put up with me?" she asked, trying to lighten the mood.

"I've told you once. You're a part of me."

Mattie reached up a trembling hand to touch his hard jaw. "You are so special."

Joe fought not to press his lips to her palm, his eyes closed on a wave of intense emotion. "This is getting disgustingly sentimental," he muttered thickly, drawing carefully away. "Don't think all this sweet talk is going to get you out of shoveling us out of here."

Mattie noticed Joe drawing away from her for the first time and felt something knot inside her. He had said it didn't matter, but . . .

Afraid to continue that train of thought any further, Mattie followed his lead.

"I think there must be a more democratic way to decide who should shovel us out of here," she protested mildly.

Joe raised one brow interestedly. "Oh?"

Mattie nodded solemnly. "I propose a snowball fight. Fast, dirty and decisive."

Joe raised the other brow. "A snowball fight? I'm going to cream you!"

Mattie regarded him haughtily. "Grab your coat, Ryan. And prepare to meet your master."

Joe laughed and loped into the living room to get their coats. Mattie watched him go with a melting tenderness in her eyes. She had to learn to trust again, she thought sternly. Joe meant so much to her. She could not, would not drive him away with her doubts and fears. He had said it didn't matter what her foster father had done to her. No, she corrected herself thoughtfully. He hadn't said it didn't matter. He had said it didn't change the way he felt about her.

Mattie was mulling over the implications of this when Joe came back into the kitchen, interrupting her thoughts. He was frowning while dangling her rather thin coat from one strong hand.

"Mattie," he began doubtfully.

"Yes, Joe?"

"This coat is much too thin. I don't want you to catch cold," he told her solemnly.

"No, Joe," Mattie agreed with suspicious submissiveness.

"You can wear mine," he determined cheerfully, bundling her ruthlessly into his huge wool coat.

Mattie, feeling very much like a little girl playing dress-up, studied the hem of the coat, where it lay on the floor. "Isn't it a little—" she waved her arms expressively, six inches of material dangling past her fingertips "—big?"

Another time, Joe would have laughed. She looked ridiculous in his coat, lost in the sheer bulk of the garment. But right now he was overwhelmed with a wave of emotion and a fierce desire to protect her from harm. His Mattie would never know a moment's pain again, he determined grimly. Not as long as he had breath in his body would she be hurt again.

Swallowing past a suddenly tight throat, Joe strived for some semblance of normality. "I've got a better idea. Give me the coat."

Mattie gladly divested herself of the cumbersome garment and followed Joe at a trot as he grabbed her hand and pulled her into the bedroom. Stopping before a beautiful pine chest of drawers, Joe released her hand to search through its contents. Throwing clothing around with blatant disregard, he asked idly, "Why are you panting?"

Mattie regarded him incredulously, thinking of the forced march from the kitchen. "Excitement," she answered dryly.

When Joe just looked blank, she burst out laughing. "Well, honestly, Joe! Look at your legs."

Joe studied his legs obediently.

"Now look at mine."

He studied her legs with considerably more interest.

"Notice any difference?" Mattie prompted.

Joe nodded vigorously, his eyes still on her limbs. "Yours are prettier."

Mattie was nonplussed. She had never allowed any man close enough to make a comment on her legs, and she certainly wasn't in the habit of studying them herself. Did she really have pretty legs?

"What else?" she demanded hurriedly, strangely frightened by the feeling Joe's admiration evoked.

"Softer."

Mattie swallowed. "The point I'm trying to make is that your legs are longer than mine. You have legs all the way up to your ears! That means that you walk faster than I do."

"All the way up to my ears?" Joe repeated incredulously.

"Close enough," Mattie insisted vaguely. "So *naturally* when you drag me along behind you I'm bound to get out of breath."

Joe studied her for one more minute, shrugged resignedly and turned back to the chest of drawers.

"Aha!" he muttered, triumphantly pulling a sweatshirt from the depths of a drawer.

At least, Mattie *thought* it was a sweatshirt. It looked big enough to comfortably house a family of six and their pet walrus. It was a funny green color. A funny *putrid* green color, with white lettering across the front.

"This will keep you warm," Joe told her cheerfully, pulling it over her head and forcing her arms into the sleeves. "This is my sweatshirt from my college football team."

"You want me to wear this?" Mattie questioned warily, holding the shirt away from her body as if it carried some horrible disease.

Joe didn't seem to notice, however, rummaging through the same drawer for a pair of white cotton socks, which he just as efficiently placed onto her small hands.

"Uh, Joe..."

"And the pièce de résistance—" Joe intoned enthusiastically, pulling a purple baseball cap over her ears "—a hat to keep you warm."

Mattie peeked out from underneath the bill that rested on her nose, looking for all the world like a Salvation Army reject.

Joe hustled her into her own jacket, put on his coat and led her from the cabin. "Now, aren't you toasty warm?" he demanded happily.

Mattie ran into the doorframe she was unable to see because of the hat and said nothing.

"You're also," Joe announced grandly, "a perfect target." He swept up a handful of snow, packed it into a loose ball and threw it at the only visible part of Mattie...her chin.

From beneath the oversize hat, Mattie didn't even see it coming, but she felt it as it oozed with frozen slowness past the neck of the sweatshirt. She shot Joe a killing glare from beneath the hat.

"It was nice knowing you, Joe," she told him glibly, scooping up a handful of snow and throwing it in his face.

Joe let out a roaring protest and the fight was on. Mattie never bothered to run for cover. She stood her ground, scooping up handfuls of snow like a windmill gone out of control and being pelted by Joe's unrelenting attack. Breathless and laughing, she finally decided that some subterfuge was called for if she was to win this particular battle.

Spinning around, Mattie dashed toward a copse of trees, feeling Joe's continued attack as snowballs pelting her back.

"I love it," Joe gloated over her retreating form. "The enemy runs, the victor—"

His words halted abruptly as Mattie executed an unbelievably realistic skid in the snow and dropped to the ground to lie still and silent.

"Mattie?" Joe raced toward her, his face taut with concern. Reaching her side, he dropped to his knees in the snow, his hand touching her face gently.

"Mattie? Sweetheart?"

Mattie kept her eyes shut as her hands stretched surreptitiously at her sides, gathering fistfuls of snow.

Joe was really concerned now, whipping the horrid purple hat from her head to check for what he was sure must be an awful, gaping wound.

"Sweetheart, please wake up. Please be okay."

The whispered litany reached Mattie and she melted inside. He sounded so worried, and his hands were moving over her so gently. Suddenly time reversed, and Mattie was back in the end zone of the Conquerors' stadium on the day that she had met Joe. Remembering her reaction then, Mattie almost smiled. Her hands loosened on the snowballs she had fashioned, and her eyes opened.

Joe breathed a sigh of relief as his eyes met hers. "Thank God! Tell me where it hurts, Mattie?"

Mattie smiled quietly into his eyes, and one cold hand rose to caress his cheek. "Nowhere, Joe. The hurt's almost gone now."

Six

_____

Hey, Ryan, where were you yesterday?"

Through the usual roar in the locker room, Joe barely heard the question Coach Rusky directed at him. Certainly he had no intention of answering it. He concentrated on lacing his shoes and pretended that he hadn't heard.

Unfortunately Bill Jackson had. "Oh, Joe was probably with his lady friend," he began tauntingly.

"Lady friend?" K.C., a wide receiver, picked up the thread of the conversation. "Why, Joe ol' buddy, you have a lady friend you're not telling us about?"

The guys on the team loved nothing better than to tease. Knowing this, and realizing they meant no harm, Joe could ignore them. He had more important things on his mind, anyway. Like where he had been yesterday and what Mattie had told him at the cabin a week ago.

Bill Jackson stepped back into the conversation, not ready to give up on the chance to get some friendly revenge for what had happened in the locker room. "Does Ryan have a lady friend?" He repeated loudly, joking. "My goodness, does he have a lady friend! I met her myself, right here. 'Course, old Joe never did explain why he had her in the locker room after hours—" several loud guffaws greeted this comment "—but let me tell you, she was one sweet little thing. Why I could start at her toes and work myself all the way up to her—"

"Shut up, Bill." Joe's voice was frighteningly soft, emphasizing the anger he was fighting.

"Aw, come on, Joe. The guys want to hear about sweet little Mattie."

"Shut up before I make you shut up." The flat warning brought instant silence to the rowdy locker room as Joe's teammates sensed the danger brewing between the two men.

"My goodness," Bill marveled, still obliviously having fun, "this one's really got you by the b—"

"I suggest you do what Joe told you to and shut up, Bill." It was Freight Dumbronkowski's voice that halted Jackson's obscene comment, and all eyes turned to him. "Before I get it in my mind to remove your vocal cords myself."

Bill Jackson, a six-foot-four, 240-pound defensive end, paled at the comment. "Hey, listen Freight, I didn't mean nothin' by it."

"You never mean anything, Bill. Why don't you just keep your mouth shut until you do."

"Sure, Freight. Sure," Bill agreed quickly, backing away. "Joe, I'm sorry about what I said. I was just joking."

Joe unclenched his teeth long enough to mutter a reluctant, "That's okay, Bill. Just don't—"

"I won't," Bill agreed fervently, shooting a quick glance toward the hulking shadow of Dumbronkowski.

The normal roar of the Conquerors' locker room resumed as Bill Jackson left the room. Joe's eyes met Freight's questioningly.

Freight's response was quiet. "There are some things a man doesn't joke about."

Joe smiled a little. "Yeah."

Freight turned and left the room to pass that comment on to Bill Jackson, and Joe once again concentrated on his shoe laces. He stared at them intently, but he was remembering yesterday....

He had gone to see Dr. James Wright because he wanted to help Mattie. Dr. Wright was a psychologist, a noted sex therapist. Joe needed to know how to stop Mattie's hurt, how to make her stop blaming herself for wanting love.

Joe sat facing the calm direct gaze of a man barely five years his senior and began steadily, "I have a friend who was sexually abused as a child."

"Sexual abuse is very traumatic for a child," Dr. Wright murmured with professional expressionlessness.

"It also makes it damn near impossible to attain any kind of physical intimacy again," Joe stated flatly.

"Is that the problem? Are you afraid to get close to anyone?"

Joe's eyes met his blankly. "Dr. Wright, I'm not—"

"I'm not making any judgments. You are actively seeking help. Hopefully, what we discuss here can help you—"

"Doctor, my friend's name is Mattie," Joe broke in quietly. "She's very special to me. I don't have time to play games."

Jim's expression showed chagrin, and he smiled self-mockingly. "Sorry. Occupational hazard. When you said 'friend' I assumed..." he said, sighing. "Tell me about Mattie."

"It will go no further than this room," Joe stated flatly, a threat evident in his tone.

Jim did not take offense. "Of course not."

In a grim, harsh monotone, Joe relayed the bare facts of Mattie's childhood.

"It's not as uncommon as we would like to think, this sexual abuse of children," Jim remarked softly when Joe had finished.

"I know that now," Joe's voice carried a violent condemnation. "You should see her, Dr. Wright. She's afraid to get close to anyone or anything. It's as if she expects it to turn on her, to hurt her."

"And you?" Jim probed. "Is she afraid to get close to you?"

"In the beginning she was. Even now, sometimes I say something that triggers off something in her head and she runs."

"But not always?"

"What?"

"She doesn't always run from you. I mean, she trusted you enough to tell you about her childhood. That's a huge step for her to take. It's the first step on the road to dealing with the trauma."

"Is it?" Joe's face softened amazingly, his eyes bright.

"Healing is a slow process, Joe. Sometimes it's almost imperceptible. The most important thing you can do is to be there. If she wants to talk about it, listen to her. Sometimes, it's going to be damn hard to hear. Don't shut her out. Don't push her for more than she's ready to give."

Joe nodded abruptly. This was nothing that he hadn't known already.

"This foster father—" Jim began.

"He's dead." The words were imbued with a vicious satisfaction. Mattie would never know that Joe had tracked her foster father down to the South Texas town she had grown up in. Joe had gone after the man blindly, driven by the pain he saw in Mattie to punish him for the misery he had caused. Finding him dead had not erased the hatred, but Joe felt a certain grim justice had been served.

"You would have hurt him if he had still been living, wouldn't you have?" Jim read the implacable hatred in Joe's face, making his question more a statement.

Joe didn't even blink. "That twisted excuse for a man didn't deserve decent behavior from anybody."

"Well, that's a remarkably honest answer," Jim commended him bracingly. "Be as honest with yourself now, Joe."

"What do you mean?"

"I believe you when you say that you are Mattie's friend. But I also believe that you want a lot more from her than friendship."

Joe was silent, his jaw tight.

"Joe—"

"Can you teach me how to need less from her?" Joe broke in harshly, his eyes fierce.

"No," Jim admitted softly. "I can't. Maybe, just maybe, you can learn to *accept* less."

"I want...so much. Do you think she'll ever be able—"

"I think," Jim answered, "that you care for her enough to put her needs above your own. I think she's let you closer than anyone else. Maybe that will have to be enough."

"If—if it...happens—" Joe's face darkened with embarrassment "—is there a certain...method, a...position?"

"If it happens," Jim suggested succinctly, "experiment."

Joe ran a weary hand over his face. "Easy for you to say," he muttered. "What if I hurt her? What if I frighten her? What if she can't . . . ?"

"You tell me, Joe. What if you can't establish a physical relationship with her? What will you do then?"

"I'll always be her friend." The words grated past a rusty throat. "I'll always need to be close to her."

Jim regarded him compassionately. "And will you be able to handle that? Close, but never close enough?"

Joe answered with grim self-knowledge. "Better than I could handle a life without her at all."

"I'd like to meet her," Jim said quietly. "Maybe I could help her. Sometimes it's easier to open up with a stranger."

"I'll try," Joe promised softly. "I'll try for her. But..." he shook his head.

"If she *can't* give you what you need from her . . ." Jim began.

"Then I'll be back."

Jim Wright met his eyes questioningly.

"For those lessons on how to accept less."

Now, back in the locker room, Joe tightened his shoe-laces and got to his feet. It was time to talk to Mattie, to tell her about his visit to Jim Wright. Pray God, she didn't see it as a betrayal of her trust in him.

"Ryan."

Joe stopped and turned to face Coach Rusky in the now-empty locker room.

"One thousand for skipping practice."

The perfect end for the perfect week.

Hours later Mattie watched Joe prowl around her small cottage like an expectant father and knew that something was wrong. Joe was not a restless man. He had the unique ability to be still and completely at peace with himself and the world. Now he looked as if a war were being fought inside of him.

He had moved to her bookcase now, glancing at the various titles and fumbling through the small ornaments that decorated the shelves. The Mattie of three months ago would have been threatened by the invasion. The woman today was only worried about his restlessness, and sighed when he latched onto a framed photograph and inspected it closely.

"What's this?"

Mattie rose from the sofa to look over his shoulder. "It's a picture of a puppy," she told him a little self-consciously.

"Did you take it?" Joe turned to probe her eyes intently.

Mattie, a little unnerved, turned away. "Yes, I took it."

Joe's eyes turned back to the picture of the young English sheepdog. "Was he yours?"

"No. I never had a pet," Mattie answered flatly.

"Then why...?"

"Look, I saw this puppy on the street one day, I thought he was cute, and I took his picture. That's all," Mattie told him defensively, her shoulders hunched.

"Then rushed home and framed the picture," Joe finished softly, his eyes darkening. "Mattie, there's no shame in admitting that you liked this puppy."

Mattie said nothing and Joe pressed on. "Why don't you get a puppy of your own?"

Mattie stiffened. "It wouldn't be practical," she told him. "I'm gone all day, and a puppy like that would grow up to be huge and he'd probably run away anyway—"

"Mattie," Joe broke in gently, putting the picture down to cup her face and force her eyes to his. "Why are you afraid to care for anyone? Even for a pet?"

"You know why..." she began huskily, her lips trembling.

"Yes," Joe sighed. "I know why. You're afraid that in caring for something or someone, you give them the power to hurt you. But Mattie, don't you see," he pleaded softly, "you've already let yourself care about me. Do you think I'm going to turn on you? Do you think I would ever hurt you?"

"No! Joe, I know you wouldn't hurt me. But it's still so hard!"

Joe's thumbs moved caressingly against the soft skin of her jaw, soothing her fear. "Mattie...I skipped practice yesterday."

Mattie blinked, unsure where this was leading. "You did?"

"Yes. I went to go see a doctor. His name is James Wright."

Swift fear colored her eyes silver. "A doctor? Joe, are you sick? Is there something wrong?"

Joe drew a steadying breath. "Jim Wright is a psychologist, Mattie. He specializes in sex therapy."

Mattie searched his eyes in silence, then pulled away, turning her back on him.

"Mattie..."

"You went to talk to him about me, didn't you?" she demanded in a hard little voice. "You told him about..."

Joe sighed. "I didn't give him your address, if that's what you're thinking. Mattie, I went to see him for my sake."

"For *your* sake!" she turned to face him incredulously, her eyes hurt.

"Yes," Joe repeated slowly. "For my sake. After what you told me—"

"Oh, now I see," Mattie broke in bitterly, driven by pain and not believing a word that she said. "You were so disgusted by what I told you, having such a hard time dealing with the fact that I was someone's . . . toy—"

"Hell, yes, I'm having a hard time dealing with it!" Joe exploded. "Aren't you? I'd like to kill that man for what he put you through. I hurt for you, Mattie," Joe said, his voice breaking achingly and his eyes burning. "I hurt for *you*, not for me. I want to help you. That's why I went to see Jim Wright. I thought he could teach me what to do, what to say to help you heal. . . ."

"Oh, Joe," Mattie breathed, her eyes bright with tears and her lips trembling.

"Is it so wrong to . . . care about you this way, Mattie? To want to help you? Can you really blame me for that?"

"No Joe, I'm just not used to it. I guess I don't know how . . ." Her words drifted off despairingly.

"Let me teach you, then." Joe pleaded intently. "Let me teach you how it feels."

Mattie searched his eyes hesitantly. "No price to pay?"

"No price to pay," Joe echoed muffledly, reminded of all the prices she had paid already.

"And—and Dr. Wright?" Mattie probed.

Joe held her eyes. "Will you see him?"

Mattie flinched from the question, from the fear of having to tell a stranger about her childhood, about the ghosts she carried. "I can't," she whispered in defeat, closing her eyes against the disappointment and reproach she feared would be in Joe's face. "I'm sorry, I can't. Not . . . yet."

Amazingly, unbelievably, she felt the gentle brush of Joe's lips against her forehead. "It's all right," he whispered soothingly. "It's all right, Mattie. Just don't close me out. Don't run away from me. Between us, we can find the answers. Together we can do anything."

Mattie felt the tears that slipped from beneath her closed lids. He was so gentle, and he cared for her. For *her*, ghosts and all. "Joe, I can't keep *taking* from you. You have to let me give, too."

"Oh, Mattie," Joe said, sighing. "Can't you see what you've given me?"

Mattie shook her head soundlessly, her throat tight.

"You've given me your friendship and something I value more than anything in the world, your trust." His voice was intense. "Don't you see, you had to trust me to tell me about him."

"I did?" Mattie's voice was stunned. She hadn't thought about that before. "Yes, I did. I do. Joe, I do trust you." Her voice was shaded with wonder. "I . . . it feels good."

The simple statement shook her. It did feel good. Just as it had felt good to tell him about her childhood, as if just the telling would allow the pain to ease. Slowly she was discovering that she could use the past, build on it to make her a stronger person. The key was in dealing with it. Suddenly she knew that Joe could help her to do so as no one else in the world could.

Seven

"Tell me about Cole and Jassy."

Mattie and Joe were on their way to the Barons' ranch, where they would spend the night before going on to Joe's home for the Christmas holidays.

Joe gave in to Mattie's request easily. "Okay, what do you want to know?"

"Everything," Mattie answered expansively, her eyes dancing. "How did you meet and how long have you been friends and how long has it been since you've seen them. What are they like and what do they do and..."

Mattie stopped to draw a breath into her empty lungs, and Joe jumped in.

"Okay, hold it. I'll tell you everything from the moment I was conceived. Will that do?"

Mattie shot him a quelling glare. "Talk fast, buster."

Joe laughed and began, his eyes steady on the road ahead of them. "Cole and I grew up together. Born just a couple of months apart—he's older by sixty-seven days. Our parents had been friends and neighbors for years, and there's never been a time when Cole and I didn't know each other or weren't friends. We were raised almost as brothers. I was always at his house, or he was always at mine. We went to school together, started to notice girls together." Here Joe stopped and smiled in soft remembrance. "Got drunk together for the first time."

"When the time came for us to go to college, it just seemed natural that we went to the same school. We attended the University of Texas at Austin for five years, and we both played on the football team. I was the quarterback and Cole was our star wide receiver."

"That's the guy who catches the ball," Mattie inserted blandly.

Joe turned to eye her in amazement. "That's right."

Mattie studied her nails in pretended boredom, then buffed them against her shirt. "Of course it is."

Joe grinned appreciatively and continued. "Cole and I roomed together all during college. I think I knew more about him then his own parents did and sometimes used it to my advantage."

Mattie picked up the past tense of the verb. "Did?" she repeated quietly. "Are his parents gone, too?"

Joe's face was somber. "They were with my parents when the plane went down. They were all coming back from a weekend in Dallas."

Mattie reached out to touch his hand in silent commiseration. "It must have been a very hard time for both of you."

"It was. We had been friends before, very good friends, but after our parents died..." Joe shook his head. "Well, suffice it to say that we have gone through a lot together, and we are very close."

"I'm glad you had someone," Mattie told him quietly, her eyes sad. "I'm glad that Cole was there to help you through that."

Joe gripped her hand gently. "After we graduated Cole couldn't wait to get back to his ranch. He said he would feel closer to his parents there. But, Mattie, he had changed. I could almost see it happening, but I couldn't do anything to stop it."

"Changed how?" Mattie probed.

Joe shrugged uneasily. "He began to draw away from people. It was as if he had decided it was safer to keep his distance, not to care about anything or anyone so that he wouldn't be hurt if it went away. I guess it really didn't help that I had turned pro by then and didn't see as much of him as I used to."

"That's so sad," Mattie murmured. "It's so hard to open up again after you've closed yourself off. It takes something or someone very, very special to make you even try."

Joe swallowed past a suddenly tight throat, because he knew by the look in her eyes that she was talking about him.

"Is this where Jassy comes in?" Mattie prompted him.

Joe smiled. "Yeah, this is where Jassy comes in. Cole had spent ten years—*ten years*—learning how not to care, and then Jassy stormed his barricades, took him by the heart and made him love her."

Mattie inwardly flinched at the word "love" and asked hurriedly. "What's Jassy like?"

Joe grinned fondly, and Mattie felt something very new and totally unfamiliar in the pit of her stomach... something very like jealousy.

"Jassy is one special lady. The perfect woman for Cole. She has an IQ that goes right off the scale, a certified ge-

nius, and a heart as soft as a marshmallow. They seem to
give each other balance. Apart they are both wonderful,
warm people, but together... together they're perfect.''

Mattie mulled that over for a long time in silence, trying
to understand the concept of two people made perfect as
one. She had never seen that kind of union, never believed
in that kind of miracle. And Joe called it love.

Suddenly she began to realize that she didn't know what
love was. What Joe described as love between his friends
sounded nothing like the love that her foster father had
forced on her. Were there so many different kinds? And if
so, how was one supposed to tell the difference? Or had the
word been misused somewhere down the line? Was love not
the horror, but the beauty? She just didn't know. Suddenly, because of Joe, it was very important that she find
out because what he described between Cole and Jassy was
so incredibly close to what Mattie felt for him.... And if
what she felt for Joe was love—the good love Joe had
shown her between Marion and Jen Dumbronkowski, and
told her about between Cole and Jassy Baron—then what
was she running from?

Cole and Jassy Baron turned out to be warm, friendly
and very easy to be with. Mattie silently laughed at her own
fears and saw the satisfaction glinting in Joe's eyes as she
relaxed with his friends.

Cole was tall, his body lean and muscled, exactly as she
had pictured a Texas rancher would be. Ordinarily he was
a man that Mattie would have been uncomfortable around,
for he exuded a kind of understated sexuality that should
have been unnerving. It would have been awkward...
except that it was all directed at his beautiful, vivacious
wife, Jassy.

Joe had mentioned in the Jeep that Jassy was a certified genius, but she looked like a fashion model. She was, quite simply, stunning—a flaming redhead with the most unexpected purple eyes. But Mattie saw beneath the beauty to the sharp, inquiring mind. Jassy's life couldn't have been so easy, either, she thought perceptively. Such an intimidating intelligence must have chased countless people away from her, people she had wanted to stay.

She seemed happy with Cole. More than happy—contented. Mattie, with her new insight on friendship, realized that Cole and Jassy were friends as well as lovers. She hadn't realized the two relationships could coexist. She watched the couple with a kind of bewildered yearning, and Joe watched Mattie with a melting tenderness and buried hope.

The Barons were obviously delighted to see Joe again. It had apparently been quite a while since his last visit. At least three months, Mattie knew for sure, because she and Joe hadn't been apart for any length of time since the day they met.

Over dinner, they fell into a lively discussion about Joe's ranch, which Cole apparently looked after for Joe during the football season. Mattie listened with genuine interest as they discussed herd movement, pastures and beef prices. Joe seemed like a different man here, at home in the country. He appeared to have overcome his reluctance to live on the ranch after his parents' death, and Mattie realized for the first time that this was indeed where he belonged.

"I guess you'll be happy to concentrate only on your own ranch once Joe retires, right, Cole?" she asked, carried along by her train of thought. "You have quite a bit of land yourself."

She was a little taken aback by the way both Cole and Jassy swung around to study Joe incredulously.

"Retire?" Cole repeated blankly. "Are you going to retire, Joe?"

Joe gave a little half smile. "At the end of this season," he confirmed. "I'm coming home."

"That's wonderful!" Jassy broke in enthusiastically. "I remember once you told us that you wouldn't quit football until you found—" She broke off suddenly as Joe's eyes warned her into silence.

Mattie wondered at the thoughtful gaze Jassy directed her way, but dismissed the thought as Cole continued.

"I'm going to have you for a full-time neighbor again! I can't wait. It's going to be just like old times."

"Not quite old times," Jassy inserted sweetly. "I'm here now, remember? No more double dating in the hayloft."

Cole's eyes turned to Joe accusingly. "Did you tell her about . . . ?"

"How about we exchange presents now?" Joe suggested rising rather hastily from the dinner table.

They moved into the living room, where a huge Christmas tree reached toward the ceiling, and the banter continued. Mattie and Joe had gone shopping the week before for the present they intended to give the Barons, and Mattie had insisted on paying for half. It was a Jacuzzi attachment for their bathtub, and Joe had insisted that they would put it to good use. Mattie was beginning to suspect that he was right.

Jassy, in turn, handed Joe a rather flat package, gaily wrapped. "I wanted to paint something you valued most in the world. Maybe I should have waited awhile." Her eyes moved to Mattie.

Joe met her gaze in level understanding. "Maybe next year," he told her quietly.

"You paint?" Mattie picked up on that part of the exchange eagerly. "How wonderful! I've tried, you know, but I just can't seem to get the hang of it."

"On the other hand, I couldn't create the magic you do with your camera, Mattie Grey," Jassy returned admiringly. "So we're even."

"You've seen my work?" Mattie was honestly surprised.

"It's hard *not* to see your work," Jassy returned. "Your pictures are in practically every magazine from *Arizona Highways* to *Sports Illustrated*."

Mattie shifted awkwardly, a little uneasy with the honest admiration, and her eyes fell on the painting Joe had just unveiled. She gasped softly at the sheer beauty of what she realized at once must be a part of his ranch. Joe was studying it reverently, and Mattie somehow knew that the setting had a particular meaning to him. She didn't even look at the artist's signature before her eyes flew to Jassy's.

"You're Jasamine Creig," she told her disbelievingly. The painting, being a Jasamine Creig, was worth thousands, but it was the caring that went into it that gave it its real value.

Jassy smiled a little. "That's the name I work under. I much prefer being Jassy Baron."

"I attended your last show," Mattie continued quietly. "Your work is so touching. Every painting seemed to have something to say to me."

It was Jassy's turn to become a little flustered, while both men looked on at their women with almost identical expressions of smugness.

Jassy and Mattie didn't notice, however, and fell into a lively discussion about places they had seen and captured on canvas and film, respectively. Mattie felt the distance she had always maintained with others melting away, and she realized with an aching rush of joy that she and Jassy could be friends. This was something else Joe had given her.... Her eyes instinctively moved to seek him out and she found his gaze on her, warm and tender and caring. Mattie had never felt so happy as she felt in that moment. Christmas, she discovered, was a holiday of the heart.

They talked for an hour more, the four of them delighting in one another's company. They seemed to mesh somehow, complement each other, and by the time the evening was over they were well on their way to a lasting friendship. It was Jassy who bowed out of the conversation first.

Groaning comically, she rose to her feet. "I have to do the dishes now, or they just won't get done. Our housekeeper, Juana, is off for the holidays," she explained for Joe and Mattie's benefit.

Mattie jumped instantly to her feet. "Let me help you."

Jassy shook her head, but it was Cole who issued the denial. "Sorry, Mattie, that's my job."

"No," Jassy protested laughingly. "You're off the hook tonight, Cole. You stay here and entertain our guests. I'll wash *and* dry tonight."

"Sweetheart . . ." Cole began protestingly.

Jassy grinned cheekily. "You can make it up to me later," she told him softly. "In the Jacuzzi."

Mattie turned six shades of red while Cole's eyes flamed seductively. "You're on."

Jassy swung from the room with a wink, and Cole's eyes followed her the entire way.

It was Joe who brought his attention back to them with a question about the ranch. They picked up their conversation where they had left off earlier. Mattie sat quietly, not really listening to the words they spoke but observing the warmth between them. They obviously shared a genuine caring for each other.

They were both so open to other people, she thought bewilderedly, feeling, not for the first time in recent weeks, how much she missed by hiding behind the walls she had erected. They seemed to invite others to come close, while all she could do was push them away. Dammit, she was tired of being alone! She had let Joe into her heart, and he had given her back a hundredfold of what she had given him. Maybe she could have it all, maybe she could have what Jassy and Cole had, if she could only exorcise the ghosts of her past.

Mattie's brain was whirling with these confused and troubled thoughts. She knew that she wouldn't find the answer tonight, not when she couldn't even think straight, so she forcefully pulled her thoughts from their inward speculation and focused once more on the conversation around them.

It took her about fifteen seconds to realize that Cole's mind was elsewhere, too. His eyes kept drifting toward the doorway, and he shifted restlessly in the loveseat he had shared with Jassy a few minutes ago. Joe was watching him with a knowing amusement, his mouth quirked as he waited for the next move.

Mattie watched them both, bewildered. What kind of game were they playing?

Suddenly Cole jumped from his chair so abruptly that Mattie started.

"I think I'll go see if Jassy needs some help," he announced to no one in particular, already striding from the room.

The silence he left behind lasted for perhaps five seconds before Joe burst into laughter.

"Joe . . . ?" Mattie asked in confusion.

Joe was shaking with laughter, and Mattie punched his arm in frustration. "Would you stop laughing and tell me what's so funny? What's wrong with Cole? He seemed so restless. Is he sick . . . ?"

"Sixteen minutes," Joe wheezed finally, his eyes gleaming with laughter still. "He lasted sixteen minutes this time. What an improvement!"

"What are you talking about?" Mattie demanded.

"Sixteen minutes ago Jassy left this room," Joe pointed out. "Within five minutes Cole was restless. Within ten he couldn't keep his eyes away from the door. Sixteen minutes and not even politeness stopped him from going to her."

Mattie still looked perplexed.

"Mattie, it drives him crazy to be in a position where he can't see or touch Jassy!"

"That's not something to laugh about," Mattie protested indignantly. "I think it's . . . sweet."

"Of course it's sweet," Joe agreed. "But it's not what I expect from Cole Baron. The man is so independent it's intimidating. Remember what I told you on the way up here? Until Jassy came into his life, there was no one and nothing in this entire world that Cole *needed*."

Mattie considered that silently. "Another part of . . . loving, Joe?"

"Another part of loving," Joe agreed softly.

"Sweet . . ." Mattie murmured almost silently. "Still . . . sixteen minutes. Jassy must feel a little smothered."

The intimate, loving sound of laughter drifting from the kitchen was a most emphatic denial.

Hours later Cole stood quietly at the bottom of the porch steps, the cold night air cutting through his jacket as he focused on Joe's stiff back. Sighing almost silently, he crossed the front yard to lean beside Joe on the paddock fence.

Joe's eyes seemed to be focused on the horizon, but somehow Cole knew that he wasn't seeing anything but the pictures he held in his mind.

Joe turned his head slightly to acknowledge Cole's presence but did not say a word. The silence lasted quite a while before Cole finally spoke.

"Pretty night," he remarked laconically.

"Yeah," Joe agreed, his eyes narrowing in the darkness. "I thought you'd be asleep by now. We turned in long ago."

"I heard you go out about an hour ago. When you didn't come in, I thought you could use some company."

Joe smiled slightly at the unspoken friendship expressed in those two sentences. "Jassy asleep?"

"Mmm. Mattie?"

"I think she dropped off right away. She was pretty excited about meeting you. I guess it took its toll."

"She's a pretty lady, your Mattie," Cole said carefully.

"Beautiful," Joe corrected softly. "Inside and out."

"There's something in her eyes sometimes—"

"Yeah," Joe said, cutting him off abruptly. "Something we're trying to work out."

"You know," Cole began softly, "I remember you telling us once that you wouldn't retire from football and come home until you found that one special person to share your life with. I was beginning to think it wasn't going to happen for you."

Joe knew exactly what he was talking about. "I guess I was, too," he admitted. "But it only took a second. She's twined around my heart so tightly..." He sighed, and a silence stretched between them. "I need to ask you a question," Joe grated finally, his eyes wary.

"Shoot."

"It's personal."

Cole eyed him a little warily. "What are friends for?"

"You remember when you first brought Jassy here, just after you met her?"

"Of course I do," Cole recalled, his lips curving in amusement. "You dropped in for an unexpected visit and found her in the barn explaining aerodynamics to a horse."

Joe's own smile lasted for perhaps a quarter of a second. "She didn't love you then."

Cole drew a deep breath and held it unconsciously. "No, she didn't."

"She loves you now." It was a flat statement of fact, and Joe uttered it tonelessly.

"Yes." There was a world of contentment in that one word, and the unexpected stab of envy it produced made Joe's voice harsher than he had intended when he forced his next question.

"How did you do that? How did you make her love you?"

"Oh, Lord." Cole's voice was filled with sudden understanding. "Joe, I'm sorry. I didn't realize . . ."

"That Mattie doesn't love me?" Joe completed quietly. "She says I'm her best friend. It's not enough, Cole. I want more, everything. I want what you and Jassy have."

It was a curiously raw moment between two strong men whose emotions were rarely revealed.

"I didn't *make* Jassy love me, Joe. I don't know if it's possible to force love out of someone. I kept her with me, and she did the rest."

"You kept her with you?" Joe latched on to that. "How? How did you keep her with you?"

Cole shook his head wearily. "I don't want to talk about it, Joe. It's not something I'm proud of."

"It worked."

"But it cost me," Cole told him in a muffled voice. "It cost me three months without Jassy. It cost me a lot of pain and a lot of loneliness. I almost lost her entirely because of what I did. It was wrong."

"But it worked," Joe insisted in a low, driven tone.

"Ultimately, no," Cole said. "We talked about it later. She told me that it wasn't—what I did to hold her that brought her back to me. It was me, the man. Who I was, what I was, what I felt for her and what I made her feel. Before I go to bed each night, I thank God for bringing Jassy back to me, Joe. Because what I did almost drove her away."

"You're not going to tell me, are you?"

"No," Cole answered steadily. "I'm not going to tell you. There aren't any easy answers, not with love. I wish I could—" He broke off helplessly, unable to phrase what he wanted to say.

Joe understood without the words. "I'll take it as said, Cole. Maybe with time..."

"Love *can* grow, Joe. It doesn't have to hit like a lightning bolt. It's not any less because it grows slowly."

"Do you think Jassy loves you more than you love her?" Joe asked ironically, already knowing the answer.

"I can't imagine any one loving another person more than I love Jassy," Cole answered a little roughly. "If she loves me equally, then I'm one of the two most loved people in the world. And that's more than enough. It feels good to love, Joe. It feels like...being whole. Don't you think so?"

Joe thought of his own love for Mattie. "Yeah," he agreed softly. "It feels like...finally being whole."

"That's a hell of a lot, Joe. How much more do you want?"

Joe turned to meet his eyes steadily. "How much more can I have?"

Neither had an answer for that question. The one person who did was asleep in the house and unaware of the raw plea. Cole clasped Joe briefly on the shoulder in a gesture of understanding and silent support, then turned to the house where the woman who was his wife and lover and best friend waited. Joe turned back to the horizon, scanning the night for hope and strength.

Eight

———

Mattie fell in love with Joe's ranch at first sight. Stepping from the Jeep, she felt the most overwhelming sense of homecoming that she had ever experienced. It was as if she had been waiting all her life to come back to a place she had never been before. The wide open spaces beckoned her, the house seemed to call to her. There was welcome in the air.

She turned to Joe, her eyes meeting his exuberantly. "It's perfect, Joe. It looks like...home." She turned back to the large ranch house in front of her, studying the long porch and the old swing that shouted for someone to occupy it. She could see the house as it must have been thirty years ago, when Joe was growing up. A hundred years ago, when the land was not as hospitable as it was now. She could feel the history and the memories of the house and the land and the sky as if she had been here for a thousand years and witnessed it all.

Joe studied her enraptured expression with loving eyes, experiencing some powerful emotions of his own. Now, he thought in satisfaction, no matter what happened in the future, he would always be able to picture Mattie here, in his home, on his land, with that expression of joy and wonder on her face. Drawing a deep, cleansing breath, he looked around. He had been back to the ranch innumerable times since his parents' deaths, but for the first time he seemed to be looking at the land with eyes that sought out the living instead of the dead. It wasn't the memories of the past that haunted him now, but the dreams for the future.

"Let's go inside, Mattie. We have a lot to do before the evening."

His voice prodded her out of her reverie. "Like what?"

Joe began to lead her up the front steps. "Well, the ranch house pretty much sits empty in between visits. Cole looks after the land for me, but I could hardly ask him to stop by and clear out the cobwebs."

Mattie laughed at the image of Cole Baron, broom in hand, attacking phantom cobwebs. "Now I understand," she teased. "You didn't want company for Christmas. You wanted free maid service."

"No." Joe couldn't play along with the joke. The next few days were too important to him. "No. I wanted you, Mattie. I wanted you here in my home. You're the best person I know to face ghosts with."

Mattie's gaze held his solemnly, a little shaken that he had chosen the same metaphor of ghosts that she had been carrying in her mind. Joe was facing the memories of his parents' deaths with her. Maybe it was time for her to face, once and for all, her own demons.

She reached for his hand and squeezed gently. "Maybe we—maybe we can help each other?"

Joe tightened his hold and brought her hand to his lips. "Don't you know that we already have, Mattie?"

In the entryway, with its tall ceilings and softly glowing hardwood floors, Joe took Mattie's coat and removed his own. Holding her arm gently, he guided her into the living room off to the left of the hallway.

"Besides, I need your help with more than just the cobwebs," he told her lightly. "We've got a tree to decorate." One hand on either shoulder, he turned her to face the beautiful but small pine in front of the glass doors that led to the side porch.

Mattie swallowed, a hard little ache in her throat. "We're going to decorate a Christmas tree?"

"Sure. It's part of Christmas, you know."

"I've—" Mattie tried again. "I've never had a Christmas tree to decorate before."

Joe's hands tightened consolingly on her fragile shoulders. "Well, you do now. I can't do this alone."

"But how . . . ? When . . . ?"

"I called ahead and asked a couple of the hands to get it. See, it hasn't even been cut," he pointed out softly. "It was dug up and potted."

Mattie nodded a little helplessly. "It's so beautiful, Joe." One hand lifted tentatively to clasp his where it rested on her shoulder. "I think this Christmas is going to be beautiful, too."

Joe's mouth softened. "You bet it will, sweetheart. Because we're together, and that's always . . . beautiful."

Mattie turned to face him, curious at the emotion in his husky voice.

"Come on," Joe said bracingly, before she could give voice to the questions in her eyes. "Cobwebs first, tree later."

Mattie let the moment pass. "Okay, Joe. Let's start up-stairs."

Joe released her shoulders and led her to the second floor. He showed her the bedroom she would have during their stay, and pointed out his own room next to it.

Of course, Mattie knew it was his room before he told her. It radiated a kind of calm and solidity that she would always associate with Joe.

"Let's get started," she ordered enthusiastically, clapping her hands once. "Together or separate?"

Joe regarded her oddly. "Together, Mattie."

They worked for a couple of hours, dusting corners and making beds. Mattie actually made more out of it than there was, simply enjoying the calm routine. They broke off around two o'clock for a belated lunch, which Joe made with characteristic finesse, then searched through the attic for Christmas decorations that had long since been packed away.

Joe studied one of the dusty boxes, a faraway look in his eyes. Mattie saw and understood that he was years, not inches, away.

"Memories?" she questioned gently.

Joe brought his mind back to the present. "At least I have them," he murmured quietly, reaching to brush a streak of dust from Mattie's creamy cheek. "Let's make a few for you."

Mattie melted. Her eyes filled, her lips trembled as she unconsciously rubbed her face against the rough warmth of Joe's hand.

Joe pulled her carefully into his arms, pressing her face against his broad shoulder. "And for me, too," he whispered almost soundlessly, so Mattie couldn't hear. "Let's make some new memories for me, too."

* * *

Joe refused to let Mattie begin on the Christmas tree until she had eaten the supper he prepared for them. "You're still too thin," he told her autocratically.

Mattie rolled her eyes and complied, passing spurious praise on his culinary ability.

Joe, of course, got even by making her wash the dishes.

"A good host does not force his guest to wash dishes," Mattie observed blandly, up to her elbows in soapsuds.

"A good guest does not malign her host's cooking," Joe observed in return, placing a clutch of suds on the tip of her classical nose.

Mattie sneezed and dislodged the suds.

Finally the dishes were clean and put away, and Joe and Mattie began decorating the tree. Mattie would have dragged out all the ornaments and decorations and slapped them haphazardly on the tree, wherever it took her fancy. Joe insisted on systematic dispersal.

"First, we pop the popcorn—"

"I'm not hungry," Mattie insisted.

"Then we thread it," Joe continued, blithely ignoring her interruption. "Then we separate the ornaments according to size and color. Then we untangle the lights—"

"You should have packed them away straight the last time," Mattie told him severely, studying the tangled wires hopelessly.

Joe sighed. "I did pack them away neatly, I swear. Someone crawled up into the attic during the year and tied them into knots."

"Right," Mattie agreed disbelievingly. "There's some little man who has a full-time job going from house to house tying knots in Christmas tree lights."

"Come on, let's get busy," Joe ordered eagerly.

Mattie popped the corn while Joe separated the ornaments. Then Joe went to rescue the popcorn while Mattie unseparated the ornaments. Mattie was determined to attack the project with the same unbridled zeal she put into her photography, and Joe could do little to stop her. He did not want to stop her, he acknowledged to himself, studying her glowing, excited face as she wrapped the strings of popcorn around the tree.

Joe tackled the top half of the tree while Mattie worked on the bottom. She broke off her industrious labor every two seconds or so to offer suggestions to him.

"No, not there," she told him at one point, tugging on the cuff of his jeans.

Joe eyed her threateningly and dropped the ornament in question on her head.

Mattie giggled and went back to her half of the tree. Joe shook his head in fond exasperation.

Finally, well after the sun had set, the decorations were finished. All the ornaments were hung, the star was crowning the tree at the proper angle, the lights were untangled and in place, and Mattie sighed with pleasure.

"It's beautiful, Joe."

Joe carefully pulled her against him, her back against his chest, and wrapped his arms around her waist.

They both studied the glimmering lights and softly reflective ornaments with satisfaction.

"I'm glad they didn't cut it down," Mattie continued pensively. "I'd like to think that something from this Christmas will live on forever."

Joe's arms tightened. "Something from this Christmas will live on forever, Mattie. And I'm not just talking about the tree."

Mattie smiled softly, thinking about his words. "Next year..."

"And the year after that..."

"Christmas is a holiday of the heart," Mattie repeated her earlier revelation almost inaudibly, with even greater understanding.

"Mattie...?"

"Can I give you your gift now?" Mattie wheedled hopefully, twisting in his arms to plead with her eyes.

Joe swallowed a little thickly at the touch of her body twisting against his and released her rather abruptly. "Sure, let's exchange presents."

"Great!" Noticing nothing amiss, Mattie turned to run upstairs to her room, where she had left Joe's present.

Joe watched her disappear from sight, sighed, then went to check on his own present to her. They met back in front of the tree within sixty seconds, both clutching a gaily wrapped package. Mattie almost knocked him down with her enthusiastic rush into the room.

"I thought you said you weren't much good at this Christmas stuff?" Joe remarked teasingly, enjoying the dancing light in her eyes, as he tried to cover up the boisterous movements of the box in his arms.

"I guess I was wrong," Mattie told him happily. "It's easy."

Joe wanted to reach out and kiss her until she was gasping for air, so instead he thrust his present at her with a distinct lack of finesse.

"Me first," he insisted. "I don't know that mine can wait too long."

Mattie reached for it hesitantly, as if receiving a present was an unfamiliar thing, then she almost dropped it as the box moved in her hands.

"My God, it's alive!" she whispered.

Joe laughed and helped her open the box, his eyes intent on her face, gauging her reaction.

Mattie peeked into the box and caught her breath as two wide friendly eyes peeped back. "Oh..." The sound was almost inaudible, the light in her eyes was bright. "Oh, Joe..." She reached in and gently grasped the puppy, easing him out of the box. He immediately let out a yapping little greeting and licked her hand enthusiastically.

"It's an English sheepdog." Joe told her hesitantly, watching carefully. "He'll grow up to be pretty big, but he'll be a wonderful friend and protector for when I'm not there."

At that, Mattie's eyes flew to his in swift fear, and Joe answered soothingly. "I mean when I'm away for a little bit, that's all. He's just another friend to care for. You have room for one more now, don't you?"

Mattie's eyes misted. "He looks just like the picture at my cottage."

Joe nodded gently. "I thought you'd like a real puppy now."

"Yes! Oh thank you, Joe. I'll take such good care of him, I promise I will." Her face was sweetly earnest.

"I know that, sweetheart." Joe's eyes were tender. "You always take good care of your friends."

"I'm going to name him Rags. That's what I used to call...the picture." She looked at him a little shamefaced, but Joe only nodded approvingly.

"It's a great name. Don't you think so, Rags? Right, boy?"

Rags let out his endearing little bark, and they both laughed.

"Now yours," Mattie murmured self-consciously, wiping one lone tear from her flushed cheek. "I hope you like it." Juggling the box in one hand and Rags in the other, she managed to pass Joe's present to him. Apparently, she wasn't willing to let go of her new friend yet.

Joe held her eyes for a moment, reading the anxiety there, before he turned his attention to opening the package. Didn't she know that she had already given him the best present he could ever hope for? No, she didn't, he thought helplessly. Because he couldn't find a way to tell her without terrifying her in the process.

Joe lifted the top off the box and pulled out the book inside. No, not a book, he realized curiously, but a photo album. Opening the cover, he saw the first picture and swallowed, raised his questioning eyes to Mattie.

"I wanted to give you something you could look at always, to remind you of this last season before you retire. I—I thought it was probably a pretty important time to you. Is it all right?"

"It's wonderful," Joe told her helplessly, deeply touched by the time and thought she had put into her present. "You took all these pictures?"

"Yes," Mattie answered softly. "At the practices and a few of the games I attended without telling you."

"This one—" Joe touched the first picture reverently. "This is the first picture you took of me, that day we met."

"Yes. Just after you scored, before that man pushed you from behind. It came out pretty good, huh?"

Joe's fingers brushed against the picture softly. "Just seconds later I was lying on top of you."

Mattie didn't know what to say to that, so she quickly turned the page for him, showing him the next picture and the next. "This is from the birthday party...."

"I could tell by the pointy hat," Joe remarked dryly.

"And this is when you threw that football to the little boy in the stands."

Joe studied each picture carefully. She had truly captured the essence of his last season in the NFL, and he would treasure her present forever.

"There's only one thing missing," he told her.

Mattie's eyes flew to his. "There is? What . . . ?"

"You," he answered simply. "There's no picture of you in here."

"But I'm not . . ." she began protestingly, before Joe interrupted.

"Yes, you are. You're the biggest part of this past season for me, Mattie. The best part."

Her eyes softened, and her mouth curved. "You want a picture of . . . me?"

"Is that so incredible? I don't have one, you know." Joe's voice was gentle.

"No one has ever wanted a picture of me before," she explained in a muffled tone, avoiding his eyes.

"Well, someone does now." Joe lifted her chin and forced her eyes to meet his. "Can I have one?"

Mattie searched his eyes, looking for . . . things she didn't understand. "I'll go get my camera," she told him finally, a smile glowing in her eyes. "You can take a picture of me with Rags, in front of the tree. Okay?"

"Okay," Joe answered, returning her smile.

She was back within seconds, tearing down the stairs with that new enthusiasm that made Joe's heart turn over. She seemed to be meeting life head on finally, eager for what she would find. Dear Lord, had he done that for her?

"Here," she interrupted his thoughts, moving in close beside him to show him how the camera operated. "This is for focus, and this is what you hit to snap the picture. I've set it for the light. Okay?"

"Got it." Joe promised, taking the camera from her. "Go stand by the tree."

Mattie moved across the room, sweeping Rags into her arms along the way, and assumed her pose by the tree.

"Should I smile?" she asked anxiously.

"Do you feel like smiling?" Joe returned.

Mattie thought about that for all of a quarter of a second. "Oh, yes. I feel like smiling."

Joe caught that expression of discovered joy with one quick click of the camera. It was a look he would hold in his heart forever.

"Now my album is complete," he told her, lowering the camera.

"Do I—" Mattie broke off and studied the floor intently. "Joe, do I really mean so much to you?"

Joe's heart twisted and he crossed to her side, gently taking Rags from her arms and lowering him to the floor. Taking her face gently in his hands, he drew her shadowed eyes to his.

"Mattie," he sighed a little roughly. "Remember that first day in the park, when you looked into my eyes?"

"Yes," she answered hesitantly.

"What did you see?"

"Loneliness."

"Yes," Joe said, nodding, his thumbs caressing her skin softly. "Loneliness. What do you see when you look into my eyes now?"

Mattie met his eyes intently, then smiled. "I see my own reflection."

Joe's mouth lifted in a half smile. "A reflection of you . . . in me," he restated quietly.

Mattie's eyes widened in amazement. "Joe . . ."

"Do you know what I see in your eyes?" he continued tenderly.

"You. You see a reflection of yourself," Mattie answered slowly. "Why didn't I see that before? Why did it take me so long to understand?"

Joe bent and pressed a tender kiss on her forehead. "Because you haven't been looking at yourself, Mattie," he told her huskily, his lips brushing her sweet skin with each word. "You haven't been looking at me."

"But—"

"You've been looking at what you used to be and what you wanted me to be. Not at what we are." Each word was carefully drawn and spoken, and Joe's body tensed as he spoke them. "Are you ready to look at yourself now, sweetheart? Are you ready to look at me?"

Mattie pulled back to meet his eyes warily. "What do you want from me?" she demanded in a strained whisper. "What do you want me to see?"

"The truth, Mattie," he told intently, his eyes fierce. "I want you to see the truth. In me and in yourself. I want you to see the need, the love—"

Mattie flinched as if to pull away, and Joe's hands tightened restrainingly.

"The love, Mattie," he repeated tautly. "If you can find it in yourself, you'll find it in me."

"How can you use that word?" she demanded, appalled.

"Love?" Joe questioned, his voice rough with pain. "Because that's what this is. It's love, Mattie. And it's good."

"No," Mattie insisted weakly. "Love is—"

"This." Joe, tired of fighting with words, brought his lips down to gently cover hers. Back and forth, soft and slow, he caressed her with only his lips. "And this." Now his arms closed to bring her against him, their bodies curving together like two halves finally united.

Mattie experienced it all with stunned disbelief. It didn't hurt, she thought dazedly. It wasn't pain she felt, but the most frightening little *ache*, centered somewhere that had never ached before, in a place that had known only the touch, the violation of Frank Bowers.

"No!" She shook her head in wild denial. "No, I can't! Please, don't ask that of me! Please, let me go."

Joe held her gaze for one more tense moment, then sighed and released his hold on her.

"You never wanted to be my friend, did you, Joe?" Mattie demanded painfully. "You always wanted... something else."

"You're wrong," Joe told her steadily. "I wanted to be your friend. I just never wanted to be *only* your friend. Do you see the difference?"

"No," Mattie answered flatly. "I don't. And I don't want to." It was the fear that made her say the words, but inside she felt as if a part of her were dying.

"It won't go away," Joe said softly, holding her eyes intently. "It won't go away just because you won't see it."

The words echoed in Mattie's mind, rolling endlessly through her fear. She left the room without answering, or looking back to see Joe press the heels of his hands against his eyes, his whole body crying of defeat and fear.

She spent hours in her room, staring bleakly at the wall as the scene played itself over and over in her mind. The only clear thing was that she had run away from Joe again. He had used the word love, and she had bolted. What was she going to do? She couldn't lose Joe, not now. He was so much a part of her, so much a part of the woman she was becoming.

A price to pay... Joe had said there was no price to pay for friendship, but he had said nothing about love. She couldn't love. Love was pain and degradation. How could he offer her that and friendship in the same breath?

Unless what he called love was really caring. Like what Cole and Jassy shared. She wanted that with Joe, wanted the warmth and the laughter and the oneness. If that was what Joe meant by love.

Nine

Joe was in bed, trying to sleep when Mattie came in.

He heard the hesitant opening of the door and the sound of her light footsteps as she crossed the room. His breath caught somewhere deep in his chest.

Why had she come?

His hands knotted into fists at his sides, evidence of the steely control he exerted, as he heard her, *felt* her, stop beside his bed. Should he keep pretending to be asleep? Should he ask her what the hell she thought she was doing in his room at this hour of the morning? Should he haul her beneath him and kiss her until she couldn't remember why she had come to him in the first place?

That was definitely the most appealing. Mattie, beneath him. Hungry and passionate and soft...

His body began to tense predictably at the mental image he had conjured up, and a shudder twisted through him.

He was about to give up the pretense and open his eyes when he felt Mattie's hand reach out to brush a lock of hair from his forehead.

"Joe..."

It was not the sound of his name, but the emotion in her voice that brought his eyes open. She had sounded—he didn't know. Sad? Peaceful? Scared?

"Mattie," Joe reached to catch her hand in his and sat up in the bed. Moonlight streamed in through the window and caught them both in its glow.

"Sweetheart? Is there something wrong?" Joe's voice was full of tender concern, and his eyes studied her face intently.

Mattie shook her head silently, unable to speak past the wave of emotion consuming her. Yes, this was right. How could she ever have doubted it? Joe was the only one who could give her what she so badly needed. He had already given her more than she could ever repay. She'd just been too scared and too blind to see it.

"Mattie...?" Joe's hand tightened on hers. "Did you have a nightmare?"

"Yes." Mattie's voice trembled. "A lifetime of nightmares. I just woke up, Joe."

Joe was confused, wary and so hungry for her touch that he was afraid to look at her. After what had happened earlier, he was afraid to hope.

"Mattie—"

"Joe—"

They both broke off.

"Would you like to...go for a walk, or something?" Joe was endearingly awkward, trying to keep his eyes on her face and away from the short sheer cotton T-shirt she wore.

"Or something," Mattie agreed softly, seating herself on the bed by Joe's hips. Her hands fluttered helplessly over his bare chest. "I need to ask a big favor of you."

Joe's face softened. "Anything, Mattie. You know that."

She drew a shaky breath and closed her eyes. "I want you to...love me, Joe." Her eyes fluttered open, suspiciously bright. "I want you to *make* love to me."

Dead silence followed her husky plea. Joe's hands dropped from her face. He seemed even to have stopped breathing.

"What?" His voice was blank, rusty. "Mattie, I thought you said—"

"I did."

"Because of what happened earlier?" Joe's voice was harsh and cold.

"Yes," Mattie began hesitantly, wondering how to explain.

Joe shook his head in instinctive, violent denial, only able to fear that it would be wrong and that he would lose everything. "No!" he forced out the word. "Oh no, Mattie! I won't take your pity. I haven't sunk quite that low. Not yet."

"It's not pity! I've been thinking about this a lot, Joe," Mattie insisted quietly, her voice trembling. "I need so badly to learn about that kind of...love. I want to know what Cole and Jassy have, what Marion and Jen have. You've been around happy marriages all your life. You know what it is to love. I need to know that."

"And what if you don't find that with me?" Joe demanded harshly, his breathing ragged. "You're a virgin, dammit. What if I hurt you? Will our friendship survive that?"

Mattie met his tortured gaze with tender, trustful eyes. "You wouldn't hurt me, Joe." There was a certainty in her tone. "You would never hurt me."

Joe swallowed, lifting her hand to press it to his lips in helpless need. "No," he conceded tautly. "No, love. I would never hurt you." His lips brushed against her palm. "I would make it so good for you, Mattie."

"If it's that you don't...want me..." Mattie looked away. "I understand, Joe. Really, I do."

"Don't want you?" Joe repeated incredulously, shaking his head. "Are you crazy?"

"Then show me," Mattie pleaded shakily. "Show me about love."

"Mattie, I can't lose what you've given me. I can't lose our friendship."

"That's right, Joe," Mattie told him steadily, twisting his denial. "You can't. It's not possible. Just as I can never lose what you've given me. We're a part of each other now. Would the loving be so different?"

Joe could not deny the gentle logic, and he didn't want to try. His eyes closed as he fought to marshall his hungering senses. "We'll do it my way." His words were achingly husky as he tacitly admitted defeat. "Slow. Easy. Soft." Emerald-green eyes burned into gray, searching for acceptance.

"Yes." It was all she said, but it said everything.

Joe flipped aside the corner of the blanket, inviting her into his bed. "Come to me."

Mattie slid silently under the covers beside him, shivering as Joe carefully closed his arms around her.

Mattie caught her breath as she absorbed the shock of his hard male body against hers. They were both silent as they adjusted to the feel of their bodies together. We're so different, yet we meld so perfectly, Mattie thought in wonder. Joe's hands did not move on her, but simply held her close as he breathed deeply of her scent.

Finally, he spoke. "You don't know anything about making love, do you, sweetheart?"

Mattie experienced a frightening, slashing memory of the traumas of her childhood, before forcing the picture away. She shook her head, her cheek brushing against his hair-roughened chest.

"The only rule is that there are no rules. If something pleases you, then it's right. If something frightens you, then it's wrong. You know what feels good to you," Joe continued softly, shifting to look deeply into her eyes. "So if you touch me here—" he grasped her hand gently and raised it to his face, directing it down his jaw "—then I'll know it's okay for me to touch you, too." His large hand moved to echo the caress across her own jaw.

Mattie nodded hesitantly, a question in her eyes. "How far...?"

"All the way," Joe answered quietly, intently. "It's the only way between us."

Mattie caressed his face gently, her eyes tender. "I care for you so much."

Joe drew a deep, calming breath and closed his eyes on a wave of intense emotion. "I... care for you, too, Mattie. So much."

"Then it will be all right," she told him with husky confidence, shifting slightly to run her hand across his shoulder. "Strong shoulders..."

Joe's hands echoed the motion faithfully on her slight frame. "Delicate shoulders..."

Mattie pressed a kiss against his jaw and felt the slight rasp of his beard. "A little rough..."

Joe's lips burned against her skin. "So soft..."

Mattie's tongue peeked out daringly to taste the taut skin at the base of his neck and Joe shuddered. "Salty...and cinnamon."

"Oh God," Joe whispered shakily, his own tongue brushing against her throat as he felt himself sinking into passion. "Sweet...and cinnamon."

The exploration was soft and slow and mutual. For Mattie it was glorious to touch and be touched, to control and ignite and feel passion. When she balked, Joe encouraged, but never insisted. When she grew bold, Joe moaned in strained hunger. When she drew away in fear, he soothed and urged her back. And when he noticed her hesitation, he gave her courage.

"Mattie, there is no part of my body that you can't touch. No part of me that doesn't ache for the feel of your hands, your lips..." And for the first time in their love-making, Joe took the initiative. Holding Mattie's eyes with his, he drew her hand to his hard abdomen.

Joe's eyes closed with a shudder as he felt her hand so close...and Mattie moaned in incredulous hunger.

"No part of me that doesn't need you," Joe reiterated thickly, his eyes still closed.

But when Mattie's hands slipped down to carefully cradle the length of his masculinity, when her soft fingers moved over his hardness, Joe's body buckled uncontrollably and Mattie drew away in fear.

"I hurt you!" she cried.

"No. Oh God, no, Mattie. You pleasure me...you make me whole...please, come back to me. Please touch me again."

"You really don't mind?" she asked hesitantly, conscious of her own fears.

"I really don't mind," Joe confirmed softly, his eyes liquid warmth.

"I—I would be frightened to have you touch me . . . there," she confessed in a rush.

Joe swallowed. "Then I won't. Not unless you ask me to. Do you want to touch me now?"

Mattie did, more than anything else in the world. She wanted to hold him, to be held. Her hands moved back.

He was so big, she thought reverently, but so gentle. And the sweet seduction continued. Each touch became the sweetest kind of agony, each moan the most wild music.

When Mattie's hands encountered the hard, bare flesh of his thighs, Joe drew a rough, shaky breath, fighting to remain still beneath her exploring touch.

"So good . . . you feel so good," she whispered in awe, the words lost in his mouth as it covered hers.

But when Joe's hands slipped to the hem of her sheer T-shirt, Mattie stilled suddenly, her eyes meeting his.

"It's just that I'm a little scared." Her eyes reflected both need and vulnerability.

Joe's eyes closed in raw agony, a muscle kicking to life along his jaw. "Then we'll stop," he told her in a thick, strained tone. "I told you once—you have only to say the word."

Mattie felt the strain in herself, saw it on Joe's face and in his body. "No," she denied, brushing a fallen lock of hair from his forehead, her eyes tender and hungry and yearning. "No, don't stop. Teach me not to be afraid."

Holding his eyes with hers, Mattie sat up and slowly pulled the shirt over her head, leaving her body bare to Joe's burning gaze.

Joe stopped breathing. His muscular, gleaming chest expanded with air that he could not for the moment release. He didn't reach for her at once. He simply looked his fill at the soft, sweet curves of her body.

With a helpless groan he reached out his arms, his eyes pleading with her to come to him, to give him what he would not take. Taut and aching, he felt the wild shudder that shook her as she moved against him, trembling as their bodies brushed and meshed and entwined.

"Are you all right?" he demanded, shaking, his lips in her tumbled black curls.

Mattie nodded, her damp lashes brushing against his neck.

"Don't cry," Joe whispered, agonized. "Please, love, don't cry. We don't have to do this. We can stop now. It doesn't—"

Mattie's lips against his own stopped the flow of desperate words. "I don't want to stop. I want to be a . . . part of you. Show me how to love."

With a muffled groan Joe gave in and showed her his love. It was urgent and gentle and hard and sweet and slow. And always, always patient. Broken murmurs, softened sighs were the only sounds between them. Green eyes held gray as Joe's hands moved to Mattie's soft thighs, searching for even a hint of fear as he brushed and coaxed and teased them into parting.

"Yes?" he questioned hoarsely.

"Yes," she answered weakly.

He saw the flare of fire in her eyes as his fingers brushed against the warm, secret heart of her. He saw her lashes drift closed in pleasure as his hands grew bolder and more intimate. He did not see fear.

"Joe . . ." she breathed on a wild shudder.

"Yes," Joe repeated against the tiny swell of her abdomen as his lips brushed lower. "Just Joe. Always Joe."

Mattie's eyes flew open in stunned ecstasy as his lips replaced his fingers at the center of her thighs, building a throbbing wave of hunger higher and higher within her.

"Sweet, so damn sweet..."

Her hands tightened on his shoulders, pale against the breadth of his tan skin.

"Joe, please! It's back. You brought it back. Make it go away!"

Joe stiffened immediately, rising to meet her eyes. What had he brought back? Please, not the fear, not the memories of violation. He sought her passion glazed eyes fearfully, searching for his answer.

"I feel...empty again. Lonely, so lonely, Joe. Here." She took his hand and brought in low on her body, just above the downy curls at the apex of her thighs. "Joe, can I have you here?"

Her eyes held his with such yearning and such a blatant trust. Joe released the shuddering, pent-up breath he held.

"Yes, love. Mattie, you can have me there, inside, loving you. I'll take the emptiness away. I'll fill you with me. I promise you'll never be lonely again."

Slowly, during the passionate litany of his words, he eased into her body. A body that he had made so hot, hungry and moist for him that there was no pain, only pleasure as he sheathed himself inside. His hands continued to play with her throbbing softness, his lips brushing and nipping and suckling at the hard tips of her swollen breasts. The pitch of her arousal was such that the first thrust robbed her of breath and reason. She could only feel and move as he cradled himself within her.

Once, she gasped at the exquisite pleasure his fingers brought her, and Joe stopped moving, breathing heavily, still within her.

"Mattie?"

"More," she whispered incredulously, her eyes pleading with his. "More. All of you... in me."

"Sweetheart..." Joe trembled, and Mattie felt it within her own body. "You're so small...and tight. Are you sure?"

"So hungry. Joe, I'm so hungry for you!"

Joe began to move again, hard and deep and full within her. Mattie's body took over then. Moving, enticing, inciting him to a thrusting possession that speared the very heart of her.

"Mine," Joe whispered as he claimed her again and again. "Mine now, Mattie. A part of me..."

Together they climbed to a place neither knew existed, clinging and straining and arcing toward their final completion.

Mattie felt her body tense and shimmer, like a spring too tightly wound, and cried out at the unknown beckoning to her.

"Joe...!"

"Mattie," Joe pleaded huskily, his fingers clenching in the soft skin of her hips as he thrust more deeply inside of her. "I need you so...."

Mattie followed him over the boundary they had rushed to, clenching around him, holding him tightly within her body, determined never to be alone again.

A part of him...forever.

Their breathing gradually calmed. Mattie's trembling subsided to gentle frissons of pleasure originating from the hypnotic brush of Joe's callused fingers on her bare skin. Joe's heartbeat ceased its race and quieted to a wondering thunder.

Joe held Mattie carefully against his chest, breathing in her silken scent. She felt so right in his arms, he thought with a sigh. A part of him, and so small to hold so much of his heart and soul. Mine, he determined fiercely, unconsciously tightening his hold. *Mine.*

But she was so silent. Even during the peak of their climax she had only whispered his name. Now she lay still, barely breathing against him. What if he had not pleased her when he needed so much to please? What if all she had experienced in his arms was fear? What if he had hurt her? She was so delicate, and he was a big man.

Finally, when the silence became so oppressive that he could not stand it any longer, he spoke. "Mattie?" he whispered carefully, his lips moving in gentle caress at her temple. "Sweetheart?"

"I didn't know it would be like that." Her voice was thin and distant, her tone frighteningly blank. "How could I have known?"

Joe, in his fear, took the words as a pained reproach. Mattie, awash in the aftereffects of a totally unexpected ecstasy, was too dazed with remembered pleasure and satisfaction to notice.

It had been perfect, she thought incredulously. No, more than perfect. Joe had come into her body, as he had already come into her heart, and somehow in doing so had driven away the haunting fear of physical commitment. Joe had chased away all those years of distancing herself from the world, she thought yearningly, with his hungry, gentle possession.

Mattie could not speak, overcome by the wave of joy he brought her. All her life she had spent alone, empty, looking for a missing piece of her soul, and afraid to know where or what it was. Now she knew that it was Joe. Joe in her arms, in her body, in her mind and her heart and her soul. Finally she could feel and need.

The emotion overwhelmed her. Tears slipped unconsciously from beneath her closed lids and trailed slowly down her cheeks.

Joe froze, shards of burning pain slashing at him viciously. Words that he had never planned and never spoken clawed at his throat, and tumbled into her silky hair. He could not meet her eyes, unable to witness the regret he knew must be mirrored there.

"Mattie, listen to me," he began urgently, his tone intense.

Mattie sighed blissfully.

"If—if what happened . . . if tonight didn't please you—There are other ways, Mattie."

"Other ways," Mattie echoed faithfully, barely listening.

"Other positions," Joe clarified with an endearing awkwardness. "Other...methods." His whole body was coiled with tension.

Mattie blinked, finally coming to. "Other ways to make love?" she questioned blankly. "What do you mean?"

A muffled sound, midway between a sigh and a groan, escaped Joe. "You could . . . control the lovemaking. You could be on top and pace it any way . . ."

"Other methods?"

"I don't have to . . . possess you that way," Joe explained carefully, his eyes desperately wary. "I don't have to be . . . inside of you."

Mattie tried to raise her head to meet his eyes, but Joe would not allow it, his hand tangling in her hair to hold her against his shoulder.

"How?" She had no idea what he was so carefully not saying.

"I can use my hands," Joe continued with an aching gentleness. "My lips . . . my tongue."

"Inside of me?" Mattie began to tremble at the thought.

"Anywhere. Anywhere you want me," Joe told her quietly. "I asked Dr. Wright about it, and he said that we should experiment. Anything that you feel comfortable with, any—"

"You talked to Dr. Wright about…making love to me?" Mattie was incredulous. "You wanted me? How long have you wanted this?"

Joe tensed. Should he tell her now? Would she be frightened at the depths of his love for her? A love she still couldn't understand?

Drawing a careful breath, he told her, "I've felt this way about you since we met. I wanted you in that end zone, and I loved you at the park. But it's not only that, Mattie," he rushed to explain. "It's so much more. The friendship wasn't a lie. You are my best friend. I'm in love with you, but I also love you. Do you understand the difference? Even if we could never have this—" his hand smoothed along her shoulder to indicate what he meant "—I would still want you, want to be with you."

"Joe—" Mattie's voice was broken, and tears danced in her eyes.

"Is it okay? Do you mind so much if I love you this way?" Joe's eyes pleaded for reassurance, and Mattie gave him the only one she was capable of at that moment.

Rolling to face him, she spread her body over his, holding his eyes intently. "Kiss me, please," she whispered, her hands caressing either side of his neck. "Show me this love again."

Joe needed no second invitation. With a smothered groan of thankfulness, his lips closed on hers, taking possession again to lead her into the timeless land of passion they had found together.

The loving was different now. Joe, no longer the acquiescent partner, explored Mattie's body as if it were the last thing he would ever be allowed to do on this earth. He teased and stroked and licked and nibbled. He touched and probed and possessed, bringing Mattie to such a heightened state of arousal that she could only shiver beneath his sensuous assault.

This time when they reached their climax, Mattie did not whisper his name. She sighed it into his mouth as he scorched himself into her heart.

A long time later Mattie rose from the bed, leaving Joe still sleeping. She crossed to the door, then turned, studying his form with eyes that were lost and frightened. With a sigh, she left the room and drifted down the hallway. On her way down the main steps and into the living room, where the beautiful pine Christmas tree with its blinking lights and glittering ornaments beckoned, Mattie tried to deny the ghost that drove her.

What she had shared with Joe had been the most beautiful thing in her life. It had taken Joe to show her that her body could be touched without causing pain or fear. He had released her from her fear of sex. But the one thing Joe could not do was to take away her fear of love.

She was so confused! All of her life, Mattie had equated love with pain and degradation. Her foster father's words were branded into her mind. Joe said he loved her. But it wasn't the same. Joe's love was gentle and warm and slow. Marion Dumbronkowski loved his wife. But their love was protective and expanded with each child they had. Cole Baron loved Jassy. But their love was binding and uniting. What was Joe offering her? What was love? Mattie felt everything good and warm and gentle in her soul for Joe, but she could not label it love.

Would she ever be free of her past? And could she go to Joe if she wasn't?

No, she determined sadly. Joe deserved a woman, not a child afraid of the dark corners of her mind. A child who tried to run from ghosts and could never quite outdistance them.

Mattie swallowed painfully and closed her eyes against the blurring lights of the Christmas tree. She would pack up her fears and her ghosts. She would take Rags with her and run again. Pray God, it would be the last time.

When Joe woke up and found Mattie gone, he almost went crazy. Leaping convulsively from the bed, he barely took time to grab his jeans before he bolted out of the room.

"Mattie!" he called her name from the top of the stairs and got no response. Hurtling down the steps, he called again as loud as he could, but something deep and frightened inside of him knew he would get no answer. "Mattie?"

He searched every inch of the house, as if expecting to find her hiding in some corner. But she was gone and she had taken Rags with her.

Grabbing the phone, he punched out the Barons' number and waited impatiently for the line to be answered. Cole was probably out on the ranch somewhere, and Jassy was doubtlessly lost in one of her masterpieces. For the first time Joe wished his friend's wife weren't so dedicated to her art that she didn't even hear the phone ring. Why didn't somebody answer...?

"Hello?" Jassy's breathless tone finally interrupted his impatient thoughts.

"Jassy, it's Joe. I—"

"Oh, hi Joe. I was going to call you in a little while—"

Joe interrupted brusquely. "Jassy, have you seen Mattie?" It was a long shot, but the Barons were the only ones in the area Joe could think of who Mattie might go to.

"That's what I was going to call you about," Jassy reproved gently, drawing a muffled curse from Joe.

"Well?"

Jassy was silent for a moment to let Joe know what she thought of his attitude then, hearing his harsh breathing, relented. "She came over here very early this morning. One of your boys dropped her off. She said that there was some kind of family emergency and she had to go home."

"Oh God," Joe muttered sickly into the silence.

"She said that you were out on the ranch when the call came in and she couldn't get in touch with you, so she hitched a ride to our house."

"Is she still there?"

"No. Remember, last night Cole mentioned that he had to fly into Dallas today. Mattie flew in with him."

Joe was silent for so long that Jassy became concerned. "Joe? You're not angry, are you? She said that she really needed to go home."

"She really needed me," Joe corrected wearily. "She just doesn't know it yet."

Jassy was not dumb. "No family emergency?"

Joe sighed. "No family. So it hardly seems likely, does it?"

"I'm sorry." Jassy's words were sincere.

"Me, too."

"What are you going to do?" Jassy asked after a small silence.

"Find her," Joe answered simply. "Try to make it right again."

"Maybe she just needs some time," Jassy suggested hesitantly.

Joe remembered what Cole had told him about almost losing Jassy. He couldn't let Mattie leave him like that, not because of what he had told her or done with her last night. He had to bring her back to him, back to his friendship, if nothing else. And somehow, he had to find a way for both of them to forget last night. Because he knew, with an aching defeat, that last night was why she was running away again.

"Joe?" Jassy's concerned voice prodded him back into the present.

"There are a lot of things I can give her, Jassy," he told her tautly. "Distance isn't one of them."

He hung up before Jassy could think of an answer.

Ten

But Mattie got her distance—two months and hundreds of miles of it. She was halfway to Port Arthur by the time Joe reached her cottage. She went back to find her ghosts, to face them one last time.

For an entire week she simply walked around the town, visiting all the mistily familiar places of her childhood absorbing all the memories that assaulted her. On the eighth day she went looking for Frank Bowers, the foster father whose memory haunted her. As Joe had before her, she found that he had drowned five years ago.

Mattie felt nothing—no elation, no regret. She was curiously numb as she realized that she would never look into the man's eyes again, never confront him with what he had done to her. What had she been planning to say to him anyway, she asked herself with despair. He would have enjoyed knowing what he had done to her, to her life.

That thought brought Mattie up short. What Frank
Bowers had done to her had taken place in the space of
three years. And yet he had ruled her life, her thoughts, her
emotions for the ten years since she had last seen him.

The ghosts weren't here in Port Arthur, she realized
painfully. Here there were only streets and houses, people
from the past. The ghosts were inside of her. If that were
true, if she really did carry the ghosts within the darkest
corners of her mind, then she could eradicate them. She
had to bring them into the light of perspective, to deal with
them, accept them and banish them. For Joe's sake and for
her own.

Joe literally camped on Mattie's doorstep for three days.
He didn't eat. He didn't sleep. He could only remember
that last night with her, and the memory was like barbwire
tearing into his skin. He played with that memory
constantly, because for two months it would be all he had
of Mattie.

He somehow dragged himself into uniform for the game
that week—a play-off game, at that—only to be replaced
in the second quarter by the team's second-string quarterback.

On the sidelines Coach Rusky roared at him. "Ryan,
what the hell is wrong with you? You're playing like you're
at Scout camp. Why did you throw the damn ball?"

Joe just walked away. In truth, he didn't even hear the
coach's tirade. He was wondering what Mattie was doing
right now.

Coach Rusky stared after him blankly. "What the
hell...?"

It was Freight Dumbronkowski who provided the answer. "I haven't seen his lady around in a while, Coach. I
think she left him."

Rusky turned his steely eyes on Dumbronkowski. "You can just keep your opinions to yourself, Freight. You're still not out of trouble for that last stunt you pulled."

"Jen was in labor, Coach—" Marion began defensively.

"And you walked out in the middle of the game," Coach Rusky reminded him incredulously. "I looked up to see ten men on the field instead of the eleven I sent in. I see you running out of the stadium—in uniform. And I see the other team score a touchdown."

Marion tried to look ashamed and failed miserably.

"How is your new daughter, anyway?" Rusky demanded reluctantly.

Marion smiled joyfully and pulled out a picture.

Farther down on the bench, Joe relived that last night with Mattie again.

Mattie stepped from the car and took a deep, satisfied breath. She was home, she thought with a shining contentment. Home to Joe. Her eyes studied the ranch house quietly as Rags bound out of the car behind her. Mattie started up the front steps and Rags followed friskily.

When her knock produced no answer, Mattie turned to sweep her gaze over the land surrounding the house. Joe would be out on the ranch somewhere. She knew that the door wasn't locked—it never was. But she decided to wait for him on the porch, absorbing the crisp beauty of the February day. She would wait now for what she had waited for her whole life.

Mattie pulled herself up on the porch rail, drawing her legs up to rest her arms on her knees. Her eyes remained steady on the horizon as if she could see Joe just beyond. Rags danced around the front yard, clearly delighted with the space and clean air surrounding him. Mattie watched indulgently for a while, then allowed her attention to drift.

She returned to Joe a whole person. She had known that even before Jim Wright's confirmation two days ago.

After two months of searching through the past for that part of herself that Frank Bowers had taken, Mattie was almost ready to return to Joe. There was only one thing she needed to do first. With a firm grip on her newfound serenity, she made an appointment to see Dr. James Wright.

The appointment was scheduled for early afternoon, and the bright winter sun bathed Mattie in its glow as she faced Jim Wright. He regarded her with a well-subdued wonder, taking in the radiant calm she exuded.

"You're not what I expected," he told her frankly.

Mattie smiled wryly. "Me, either," she told him with stark honesty. "I've changed since Joe came to see you, grown."

Jim studied her cautiously. "He told you about that?"

Mattie nodded, her eyes loving as she thought of Joe. "He told me."

"You know," Jim began solemnly, "in my work, I've managed to help a lot of people come to terms with themselves, to find a semblance of peace. Sometimes, I can't do that. Sometimes, a patient can't find that peace even with my help. And sometimes," he finished deliberately, "very rare ones will find it all by themselves . . . as you have."

Mattie shook her head. "Not by myself, doctor. Joe Ryan gets the credit for this. I would have been too afraid to try without him. Too frightened of what I would have found."

"Have you told Joe this?"

"I'm on my way to him now."

Jim met her eyes bluntly. "Why are you here now?"

For the first time Mattie's eyes avoid his. "I...I guess I just wanted to be sure that what I've found is real."

Jim nodded with calm understanding. "Tell me what you've found," he invited easily.

Mattie needed no further encouragement. She was almost bursting with the hard-won knowledge she had acquired.

"I learned that all those ghosts I went back to Port Arthur to wrestle with weren't there. I learned that they were inside of me, that I had carried them with me all these years like a millstone around my soul. Once I accepted that..." Her voice drifted off, her eyes briefly unfocused.

Jim leaned forward, his eyes intent. "Once you accepted that...?" he prompted.

Mattie met his eyes squarely. "Once I let them go, I was free. Free of the past, free for the future. What happened to me will always be a part of me, but not the biggest part. I have a whole life to live, and I intend to live it to the fullest, without fear, without the past coloring the future."

Jim nodded with deep satisfaction. "Yes."

Mattie regarded him quietly. "It's really that simple?"

"It always was, Mattie," Jim promised her calmly. "But that wasn't the hardest thing for you to accept, was it?"

Mattie was a little nonplussed by his perception. "No," she conceded. "I figured that part out the first week I was gone. It was...something else that held me back."

"And have you figured out...something else?"

"It's love," she told him flatly. "I've been so terrified of that word. All my life I've associated it with loss and pain and...degradation. My parents 'loved' me, but they left me. My foster father 'loved' me, but he hurt me. When Joe came into my life, when he showed me that other kind of love, a good kind of love, I was so—confused. I didn't understand..."

"Didn't understand what, Mattie?"

"I didn't understand that there is only one kind of love," she told him slowly. "The good kind. All the rest is make-believe, unreal. Love isn't the word people use. It's the emotion behind it. It's what I feel for Joe."

And Mattie, lost in the memory of that discovery, didn't notice that Rags had wandered off.

Joe gave the wrench one more tight turn, then cursed a blue streak when it slipped and crushed his thumb against the engine he was working on.

In the two months since Mattie had gone, he had lost more weight than he could afford to and it showed. He looked haggard, tired, and all the joy had gone from his eyes. He felt emptier than he had ever felt in his entire life, as if the happiness Mattie brought to him had simply made more room for the despair when she had gone. She had taken the biggest part of him with her. He wondered if she knew that and if he would ever get it back.

Two months since he had held her, touched her, loved her, he thought achingly. Two months of fear and pain and sadness. Two months of searching and hoping and dying a little inside each day. Two months without Mattie....

Joe was so lost in his despairing thoughts that he didn't even hear the barking at first. When it finally did register, he thought nothing of it. There were several working dogs on the ranch. Only when Rags danced joyously into sight, scampering up to him to tug on the leg of his jeans, Joe allowed himself to hope.

"Rags?" Joe's voice was thick and disbelieving.

The dog stared up at him with the comically endearing expression that had so captured Mattie's heart.

Mattie....

Joe bent slowly, reaching out to touch Rags awkwardly.

"Did Mattie bring you here?" he asked, stunned. "Is Mattie...home?"

Rags barked once in answer as he recognized Mattie's name.

Joe threw the wrench aside. "Take me to Mattie, Rags," he urged intently. "Take me home to Mattie."

Rags turned and trotted off happily, heading toward the house. Joe could almost believe the puppy understood the urgent yearning in his tone. His heart pounded louder in his ears with every step he took. Pounded for Mattie....

Joe froze as the house came into sight, his form hidden in the shadow of a towering evergreen. Mattie was there. Curled up on the porch railing, with her back propped against the corner column.

Rags ran on ahead, unaware of the fierce tide of emotion that seemed to cripple Joe who remained just out of sight. Mattie hopped off the railing and went down the steps to meet her errant companion, and Joe could hear her sweet, scolding voice as she playfully berated the puppy.

"Where have you been, young man? Leaving me alone like that! Why, what if a six-foot squirrel had come along and attacked me? They grow 'em big here in Texas, you know. Who would have protected me then?"

"I ran off the last of the six-foot squirrels. You're in no danger here."

Joe's husky voice brought Mattie's head up sharply. She had not heard him crossing the yard while she was playing with Rags.

Her lips formed Joe's name, but no sound emerged. Their eyes held for long seconds, a wary joy in each, before the contact was broken to allow a wider perusal.

Mattie noted Joe's weight loss, her eyes taking in the thrust of his hip bones through his jeans. He looked like he had been driving himself for weeks without rest. New lines scored beside an unfamiliar grim mouth, and his eyes looked weary.

Joe saw the new confidence Mattie carried with her, the resolution and strength in her suddenly serene gaze. If Joe had lost part of himself, it seemed that Mattie had found a part. He felt a physical pain at the thought that she had done so without him.

"You look beautiful."

Mattie smiled slightly at the husky words and rose from her knees awkwardly. "So do you."

Joe gave a disbelieving snort. "I look like hell."

Mattie's smile trembled at the edges. "Besides from that," she amended.

Neither seemed to know what to say after that, and they stood there in a strained silence. Mattie thought of all that lay ahead of her, of everything she had to tell him, but the words wouldn't seem to come.

A bitter wind blew up and Mattie shivered slightly, galvanizing Joe into action.

"You're cold," he said protectively. "You should have gone on inside the house. The door isn't locked." He gestured for her to climb the steps, careful not to get too close to her.

"I wanted to wait out here," Mattie told him quietly. "I wanted to see you coming home."

Joe said nothing as he held the door for her to enter the house.

Mattie stopped dead in her tracks when she reached the doorway in the living room. Joe almost ran into her from behind, but Mattie barely noticed, her eyes riveted to the tree they had decorated for Christmas over two months ago.

She looked at him in silent demand, and Joe shifted restlessly before moving into the room.

"The tree's still up," Mattie pointed out needlessly, her mind churning with questions.

Joe was silent for a long time before he answered, his eyes on the tree. "In memory of a beautiful Christmas Eve."

They were both silent then, remembering that night and what had followed. For Mattie it was the memory of triumph over her dark past. For Joe it was a stinging condemnation of a bitter present.

"So," she tried a little desperately, "you're a full-time rancher now, huh? You really retired from football?"

"Yeah," Joe confirmed quietly, his eyes fixed intently on her from across the room. "We kept it quiet until after the Superbowl. I announced it after they gave us our rings."

Mattie nodded a little jerkily, only taking in his affirmative answer.

"You didn't watch the Superbowl, did you, Mattie?" Joe's abrupt question caught her by surprise.

"I don't even know what it is," she admitted a little shamefaced.

Joe's mouth twisted in self-derision. "I should have realized . . . It's the game we play at the end of the season to determine who the best team in the league is."

"I bet you won," Mattie said with certainty.

"The Conquerors won," Joe confirmed. "I don't know how much help I was to them. I had . . . other things on my mind."

Mattie accepted that a little helplessly, about to question further when Joe continued.

"After the game I did something I hardly ever do. I granted an interview to one of the networks. Right there in the locker room." Joe laughed derisively. "One hundred million people saw that interview, half the entire damn country. But not Mattie Grey."

"Joe . . ." Mattie reacted to the pain in his voice, but Joe didn't give her time to say more.

"I went on national television and begged you to call me. I got the worst ribbing from the guys on the team, but I didn't care because I was sure that you would call," he continued tautly. "I stayed by the phone for two days, waiting. I didn't sleep. I didn't eat. And when you didn't call, I didn't know what to do. I was so sure that you would call. It never occurred to me that you weren't watching, not for days. When I finally remembered how little you knew about football, I had already made a fool of myself. I called every hospital and police station and morgue in the state of Texas. . . ."

The driven despair in his tone almost broke Mattie's heart. The last thing in the world she ever wanted to do was hurt him, and it seemed she had done nothing else.

"Where were you?" he demanded hoarsely, his steely control gone. "After you left the ranch I camped on your doorstep for three days. One of your neighbors finally called the police. I almost got arrested. I looked everywhere for you. Called everyone you ever worked for here in Dallas, went everywhere we've ever gone together. For God's sake, where have you been for the last two months?"

"I've been in Port Arthur," she answered quietly, her eyes steady on his.

"Port Arthur?" She saw the incredulous pain cloud his eyes. "Mattie, why did you go back there?"

"Back there?" Mattie picked up immediately. "I never told you that I grew up there, Joe. How did you know?"

Joe did not answer, his face grim.

But Mattie did not need an answer. She saw it in his eyes. "You hunted him down, didn't you, Joe?" Her voice was soft with emotion.

"I hated him for what he did to you," Joe replied.

Mattie shook her head sadly. "Don't hate, Joe. You'd be giving up control of yourself."

"Are you telling me you don't hate that bastard for what he did to you?" Joe demanded harshly, his eyes blazing.

"I used to," Mattie confirmed. "But there's no point in hating a ghost, Joe. Ghosts can only hurt you if you let them. And that's what Frank Bowers is, a ghost."

"Oh, I know he's dead—" Joe began grimly.

"He's been dead for five years, and he's been haunting me for ten," Mattie told him steadily. "Because I kept him alive inside of me. I carried the ghost of Frank Bowers inside of me. I hurt myself with his memory. Well, no more." The firm resolve in Mattie's voice brought a dawning comprehension to Joe's anguished gaze. "I'm not carrying my ghosts along with me anymore, Joe. I left you to exorcise myself of them, and now I'm free."

"Isn't it true you left me because of what happened that night?" Joe corrected tautly, his eyes fierce.

Mattie thought back to that cold dawn when she had determined to leave Joe so that she might come back to him a whole woman. "Yes—" she began softly, wanting to explain, but Joe cut her off.

"I knew that," he told her quietly, his shoulders squaring as if accepting a great weight. "I knew it that morning when I woke up alone. That's the worst part about this whole thing, do you know that? Even knowing how much I frightened you, that night was the best thing that's ever happened to me. I take out the memory a hundred times a day...the way you felt in my arms, your soft skin, that sweet gasp as I came into you for the first time..." He said nothing else for a long, pain-filled moment, then, "What now, Mattie? Have you come back to offer me friendship, or couldn't you bear to give me even that?"

"Of course I'm still your friend!" Mattie insisted, shocked at the grim hopelessness of his tone. "How could you ever doubt that? After all you've given me..." Her hand moved instinctively to her abdomen, but Joe didn't notice.

"And all I've taken," Joe interrupted. "You never seemed to realize exactly how much you changed me. I was only half a man until you came to me, haunted by my own ghosts of loss and loneliness. You filled me with laughter and lighted all those dark corners. Two months without that is more than I can take. Yes, Mattie, we'll go back to friendship. I can learn to live without the rest."

"The rest?" Mattie questioned, a rising hope choking her.

"Love." Joe grated the word. "I know you don't like that word. I guess I must have scared you silly that last night by saying it. God knows, it made you run. I wish I could find some other name for it, some name that didn't bring back all those memories...."

"Joe, I told you, I'm not carrying those ghosts around with me anymore. All I carry now is...love." She crossed the room purposefully, reaching for his large, callused hand to place it gently over the soft swell of her abdomen. "Love, Joe."

Joe met her eyes, stunned. She watched his throat work convulsively as his hand moved tentatively against her.

"A baby?" he whispered huskily, holding her eyes. "You're going to have a baby?"

Mattie nodded once, love shining from her eyes.

"But you said—Mattie, you said you couldn't have children!" Joe's voice was shaking.

"I never said that!" Mattie denied.

"You did," Joe insisted. "That day in the park. I said that you were going to make a good mother, and you said then—"

"Oh!" Mattie recalled the incident now. "I said that I *wouldn't* ever have children, not that I couldn't."

"But you sounded so sure..."

"I never thought...Joe, I thought I'd never get that close to a man." Mattie explained hesitantly, her eyes avoiding his. "Never close enough to..."

"I didn't even *think* of protecting you." Joe's voice broke on a wave of pure anguish. "That's why you came back, isn't it?"

"No!" Mattie protested hotly. "I mean, I thought you should know, but that's not why..."

"You'll marry me now." Joe's voice had never sounded so defeated, but his hand continued to move compulsively over her abdomen.

"I—I thought you weren't going to ask." Mattie's own voice was shaking.

Joe's eyes snapped open. "I'm begging you," he corrected quietly. "Marry me. Please marry me."

"I want to marry you," she told him steadily, her eyes shining with love.

Joe closed his arms around her carefully, all strength seeming to leave him as he slumped against the wall and slowly slid to the floor, taking her with him.

They stayed that way for a long time, holding each other in silence, Joe's hand caressing her body where their baby rested.

Finally, Joe broke the silence. "There are some things I want to promise you," he told her huskily.

"Joe..." The sound of his name was a denial of the need for promises.

"I'll be a good husband," he told her intently. "A good father...."

Mattie swallowed the tears that threatened. "I know you will be, Joe. I know."

Again they lapsed into silence, both lost in their own confused thoughts and thinking of the years ahead. Finally, after a long, long time, when the dusk began to shade the sky, Joe eased away from her and helped her gently to her feet.

"I'll make the arrangements for the wedding," he said quietly. "How about Saturday?"

"But that's only three days away!" Mattie reminded him breathlessly, her eyes searching his.

"There's no reason to wait, is there, Mattie?" Joe's voice was tender as his hand slipped to her abdomen. "We have our baby to think about now."

Mattie's hand covered his. "Yes, we have our baby to think about now," she agreed, a strange uneasiness seeping beneath the joy of being with Joe again. He was treating her like hundred-year-old china, when she wanted more than anything to be a woman—his woman.

"Why don't you go upstairs and lie down for a while," Joe suggested, breaking into her troubled thoughts. "You've come a long way. You must be tired."

Mattie saw the deep concern in his eyes and capitulated, telling herself that she must not worry about things that weren't there. "Okay. I guess I am kind of tired."

Mattie went on tiptoe to press a kiss against Joe's cheek, and felt the tautening of his jaw against her lips. Oddly disturbed, she turned toward the stairs. Stopping at the bottom, she turned back and saw Joe close his eyes and rake one hand through his hair. Maybe she wasn't imagining things after all. She almost started back to him, almost spoke, but just then Joe turned and strode from the room.

His shoulders were stiff, as if the weight of the world rested on them. Sighing, she climbed the stairs. She would talk to him later.

"Cole," Jassy began carefully, studying her husband from beneath her long lashes, "how do you feel about another egg—"

She broke the word off as the strident summons of the telephone sounded.

Cole studied her oddly, then turned his gaze to his dinner. "Another egg?" he repeated warily. "I didn't realize I'd had a first one?"

Jassy buried her head in her hands and mumbled incoherently. "Answer the phone. We'll talk afterward."

Cole gave the dinner table one more considering look, shook his head and went to answer the phone. When he hung up there was a thoughtful look in his eyes.

"Cole?"

Cole sat down next to her once more, his hand reaching for hers. "That was Joe," he told her.

Jassy sat up a little straighter. "How is he? The last time I saw him—"

"He called to invite us to his wedding," Cole interrupted softly, his eyes still concerned.

"His wedding?" Jassy echoed disbelievingly. "Oh my gosh! Mattie must be back!"

"Yes."

Jassy eyed her husband questioningly. "You don't sound too excited by all this."

"Neither did Joe," he told her flatly.

"Neither did Joe?" Jassy echoed disbelievingly. "What are you talking about? You know how much he loves Mattie. Why in the world wouldn't he be ecstatic at the thought of marrying her?"

"I don't know. The wedding is set for Saturday."

"But that's only three days away!"

"Yes. He's in a pretty big hurry for someone who didn't sound overjoyed at the prospect of marriage, isn't he?"

"Cole," Jassy grabbed his hand in concern. "There's something wrong. Joe adores Mattie. He's been wasting away without her these past two months..."

"I know, honey. I know." Cole pressed an absent-minded kiss to her palm. "But he's a grown man. He knows what he's doing."

"But—"

"If he needs me, he'll come to me," Cole interrupted. "I can't force him to share this."

"Cole, maybe he's too proud."

Cole sighed. "All right, Jassy. I'll talk to him on Saturday. Okay?"

"Okay," she agreed softly, her eyes loving. "You're a good friend, Cole."

"I'm a good lover, too," he said teasingly, his eyes loving her.

Jassy drew his hands to her body. "Prove it," she challenged in sweet seduction. "Prove it to me again."

Cole was never a man to turn down a challenge. He began pressing teasing little kisses to her skin, working his way from her temple to her shoulder with a thoroughly arousing skill. "You taste so good," he murmured distractedly. "Not at all like an egghead...."

Suddenly his lips stopped moving. Jassy felt him stiffening by degrees until he had finally pulled away enough to meet her eyes. They held each other for one taut moment before his gaze shifted back to the table.

"Another egg..." he muttered blankly. "Oh my God!" His eyes raced back to hers, searchingly intent. "How would I like another *egghead*?'' His tone begged for it to be true.

Jassy smiled lovingly. "Another egghead," she agreed, and brought his hand to her stomach.

The three days before the wedding passed in a blur for Mattie. It seemed there was so much to do, and so little time to do it in. Joe spent every minute with her from the moment she got up until the second she went to bed. It was then, though, that he quietly disappeared.

Maybe they both needed time, she thought wisely. They were going to have to adjust to the idea of being husband and wife. Time enough for the loving, she decided, as long as they had the love. Did he understand the niggling uneasiness she felt? she wondered. They had made love outside the bounds of marriage, and although she would never regret it, because he had given her so much that night, she wanted to make it right with the vows they would take. Old-fashioned but true. She wanted to belong to him in the eyes of God and the world before she belonged to him again in body. She somehow felt that Joe felt the same way, and it made her heart twist with emotion.

They had moved her things from her cottage to Joe's ranch, where Joe told her they would spend the rest of their lives together. Mattie's eyes softened at the memory of those words. She'd settled into one of the spare bedrooms where she slept soundly for two nights and dreamed of Joe.

When Saturday came she was finally at peace with herself and the world. Every moment of that day was preserved in her mind with beautiful, aching clarity: the sweet smell of the white roses Joe had arranged for in the small chapel, the sharp crispness of the air, the probing fingers of light that streamed through the stained-glass windows and reflected in rainbow prisms all around them. Jassy and Cole stood as witnesses to the vows she and Joe exchanged, and overwhelming reverence appeared in Joe's eyes as he bent to seal their marriage with the brush of his lips against hers.

Joe held her hand in a gentle grip on the drive home, as Cole and Jassy followed behind for a celebratory meal. They exchanged few words, but let the silence speak for them.

Once back at the ranch, Mattie changed from the white dress Joe had insisted on into a pair of comfortable slacks and a sweater. Jassy joined her in the kitchen to help her prepare the feast they would share. Mattie was bubbling over with happiness, laughing and bright-eyed as she and Jassy chatted over the meal preparation.

"You're really happy, aren't you?" Jassy asked quietly.

Mattie turned to her in surprise. "Yes, I'm really happy. It was a long road...but then, I imagine you know all about that."

Their eyes held in silent communication, then they both smiled.

"What about Joe?" Jassy asked softly.

"We're going to be a family now," Mattie answered, radiant joy shining in her words. "Neither of us will ever be alone again. We'll have each other and—" she hesitated for a moment "—we'll have our baby."

"You—you're going to have a baby? Oh my gosh!" Jassy's hand moved to her own abdomen, and their eyes met in sudden comprehension.

"Christmas Eve!" they murmured together, laughing.

"I can't believe...!"

"Does Cole know...?"

"This is wonderful! I'll have someone to complain to about morning sickness."

"And not being able to see your toes."

"And craving jalepeño ice cream."

They broke off, laughing, as the web of friendship tightened its hold around them.

Joe had disappeared immediately after they reached the ranch, ostensibly to change from his formal clothes into something more casual. Cole finally found Joe in his study, still in his suit, although the tie was now gone and the shirt opened. One hand was curled protectively around a half-full tumbler of neat Scotch that looked as if it hadn't been touched. He sat with his back to the door, hidden in the depths of the leather wing chair he had angled to a view of the gathering dusk.

"Is this a private party, or can anybody join in?" Cole's drawl from the doorway drew Joe's eyes from the window.

"Pull up a chair old buddy and join me in a drink."

Cole studied Joe for a second before straddling a straight-back chair beside the desk and complying with his friend's invitation.

"What are we drinking to, Joe?" Cole asked with studied idleness, studying the liquor in his glass.

"To women," Joe proposed quietly, solemnly. "And the love they bring."

They drank to that in silence that seemed to stretch and hang between them. Finally Joe spoke, his voice rusty.

"I had to keep her."

Cole sighed. "I know you did, Joe."

Again the silence fell between them, and this time it was Cole who spoke.

"Jassy's going to have a baby," he said softly. Joe flinched, but Cole didn't notice. "I can't tell you how it feels, knowing the woman you love is going to have your child." Cole's voice was colored with wonder and a shining contentment that made Joe envious.

"You don't have to tell me," he told Cole thickly. "I know."

Cole's eyes raced to Joe's, searching out the hidden truth. "A baby? Joe, is that how you're holding on to her? Is that why she married you?"

Joe smiled mirthlessly, his eyes glittering oddly. "I did you one better, Cole. You had your way of holding on to Jassy. I found my way of holding on to Mattie. It's the oldest trick in the book, you know. And I was enough of a bastard to use it." Joe drained the contents of his glass.

"Desperate enough, anyway," Cole corrected. "Did you plan to get her pregnant, Joe?"

"No," Joe grated, digging the heels of his hands into his eyes. "No. I guess I'm not that much of a bastard. I didn't think that she could—hell, I didn't think at all! I was just loving her."

A tap on the door prevented Cole from saying anything further. Jassy peeked in and announced, "Dinner's ready."

Joe's gaze held Cole's for one long second, and Cole nodded imperceptibly. When they left the room together, they left the conversation behind.

Hours later, after the dinner was finished and Jassy and Cole had left, Mattie stood in the doorway of the study looking at Joe. He seemed to be lost to her, though more than anything she needed to have him with her. She knew for certain now that there was something wrong. It wasn't just a desire to make things right with their marriage vows that held Joe away from her, there was something hurting him. She had to help him, to bring him peace as he had brought it to her.

"Joe," she sighed his name, and brought him from his reverie. "Are you coming to bed?"

His face blanched, and his body trembled.

"Joe?" Mattie repeated, shocked by the reaction, moving into the room to his side. She pressed against him, closing her arms around him as if in doing this she could absorb the pain she knew he felt.

"I didn't know if you'd...want that," he told her finally, his eyes burning as he cherished the feel of her against him.

"Not want it?" she repeated incredulously. "I've spent two months walking around, empty. Craving your touch, the feel of you...inside of me—"

"Mattie!" Joe groaned, his whole body tightening and taut.

"I have your baby...here." She brought his hand to her body and pressed hard, so that he could feel the swell of his baby. "But it's not the same as being full with you!"

"You want me... You really...?"

Mattie's hand covered his and moved it downward to the juncture of her thighs, where the heat and aching for his touch was tangible. "Don't you want to be here, Joe?" she demanded tautly, her muscles clenching to close around his hand.

"Oh, God!" Joe's fingers moved spasmodically, caressing and arousing and worshipping.

"Come to bed with me," Mattie whispered again, arching into his touch. "Make love with me."

"Yes," Joe gritted out hungrily. "Now, Mattie. Let me touch you now."

Mattie felt the iron-hard evidence of his need thrusting into the cradle of her hips through the confines of their clothes and moaned breathlessly. "Can you...ah, Joe! Can you make it to the bedroom?"

"No..." Joe's hands had already unzipped her slacks, and his hand slipped inside to find the hot moist throbbing he had aroused. "So sweet..." he whispered, caressing the flowering bud until Mattie's legs gave out and she began to sink to the floor.

"Touch you..." she told him hungrily. "I want to touch you, too."

"Can't stop... I can't even stop to get my clothes off!"

"Let me..." Mattie pleaded helplessly, her thighs shifting and tautening as she melted further into the heady passion he aroused in her.

Within seconds they were naked. Mattie's skin was almost painfully sensitized to the feel of the soft carpet brushing against her back and the wiry hair on Joe's chest caressing her breasts. She felt him everywhere, she thought dazedly. Inside and out, she felt his heat, his hardness, his need. She could only writhe as he went into her, taking him deeper and deeper into her body, as the beauty of the act of love brought tears to her eyes.

"I love you so much!" she cried on the crest of their passion.

Joe trembled, stopped breathing and released his iron control. "Love you..." he whispered back, his lips moving against hers with every word. "Belong to you..."

It could have been hours later when they finally moved. Mattie stretched luxuriously against Joe, feeling him in every muscle and sinew.

"My God!" Joe muttered, stunned. "On the floor! I couldn't even control myself long enough to do it right."

Mattie snuggled closer, laughing silently.

"I've got news for you, Joe. If it had gotten any 'righter,' I would have passed out."

Joe didn't even seem to hear her. "It won't always be like this," he told her urgently, his eyes desperately wary. "I can control what I feel. You won't always be obligated—"

"Obligated!" Mattie repeated, stunned. "You still don't understand, do you, Joe?" She tried to draw away, but Joe's hard arms closed on her and urged her back against him. "You're a part of me. I love you."

Joe flinched, and Mattie rolled on top of him, pinning him beneath her. "Did you hear me? I love you. It's not a word I take lightly. I love you. Don't you see? I've always loved you! I called it friendship, because I knew friendship could be good. I didn't know love could be. I thought love could only hurt, and what I felt for you *healed*."

"The baby..." Joe began.

"Yes, the baby. I love our baby, too, Joe. But that's not why I came back. I knew about the baby a month ago—"

"A month ago?" Joe's shocked question made her smile.

"There are some pretty definite signs, you know. Maybe I wasn't a hundred percent sure, but almost. And I was happy, Joe. Ecstatic."

"Mattie—"

"But I didn't come back to you then, Joe. I could have, if it was only for the baby. But I was determined to come back to you a whole woman, without ghosts, without the past hanging over us. You deserved so much more than the frightened child I was when I left you."

"Oh, sweetheart." Joe choked on the words as he read the love in her eyes.

"I'm coming to you a woman, Joe. Not because of the baby, but because I love you. The child you met is gone. Do you want the woman she's become?"

"Yes...oh, God, yes. Mattie, I love you." Joe's voice was shaking with emotion, the love he spoke of shining unashamedly in his emerald eyes.

"And you don't mind about the baby?" she asked solemnly.

"Mind?" Joe repeated incredulously. "Are you nuts?"

"Possibly," Mattie conceded, smiling at him until Joe's face turned grave again.

"Mattie, have you seen a doctor?"

She smiled wryly. "Several."

Joe immediately panicked. "Several? What do you mean, several? Is there something wrong? Something you haven't told me?"

"Stop worrying, Daddy," she told him gently. "I only meant that I have been to see two doctors. One about the baby—who is perfectly healthy," she stressed. "And Dr. Wright."

"Dr. Wright? Jim Wright?"

"The same," Mattie confirmed. "I guess I needed to test my newfound maturity on someone."

Joe pressed a soft kiss to the corner of her mouth. "I couldn't bear to lose you now, Mattie. Are you sure about the baby?"

"I'm sure," she interrupted firmly. "We're both fine. You won't lose me. Not ever. I'm a part of you, remember? And you're a part of me." She pressed his hand to her heart. "You've filled up all the empty spaces, Joe, and taken away the scars. I love you more than anything else in this world. Love, Joe. The good love. The only love."

Joe's eyes glittered with what suspiciously looked like tears. "The only love," he repeated softly, his arms tightening on her. "The only love."

Six months, three weeks and two days later, the Barons and the Ryans met on the steps of the hospital. Mattie and Jassy looked at each other and burst into laughter. Cole and Joe momentarily abandoned their wives to prop each other up. It was a toss-up as to which one of them was the palest.

Two hours later Joshua Cole Baron was born. Cole waited until he had seen his wife and child before he passed out.

A half an hour after that, Amanda Leigh Ryan made her appearance. Strictly in the interests of equality, Joe passed out, too.

Silhouette Desire

COMING NEXT MONTH

BRIGHT RIVER—Doreen Owens Malek
Jessica's father had thought that Jack Chabrol had been an unacceptable suitor for a daughter of Bright River's wealthiest family. Could love temper Jack's bitterness when fate brought Jessica back?

BETTING MAN—Robin Elliott
Kate Jennings could make book on the fact that Griff Hayden was perfect for her ad campaign. Griff was determined to convince her that all bets were off when it came to love.

COME FLY WITH ME—Sherryl Woods
Who was that man following Lindsay Tabor around Los Angeles Airport? However preoccupied Lindsay may have been, Mark Channing wasn't a man she could easily ignore.

CHOCOLATE DREAMS—Marie Nicole
Keith Calloway was a man with a mission, and satisfying the world's cocoa cravings was priority number one. But vivacious Terri McKay quickly had this serious-minded man dreaming of forbidden treats.

GREAT EXPECTATIONS—Amanda Lee
Megan couldn't share her secret with anyone, least of all Greg Alexander. Her project was too close to bearing fruit to blow her cover—yet she knew Greg could deliver the dream of a lifetime.

SPELLBOUND—Joyce Thies
According to Denise Palmer, Ph.D., Taggart Bradshaw was a stress-prone type A and therefore Mr. Wrong for her. So why was Taggart bent on showing Denise just how right he could be?

AVAILABLE NOW:

Breathtaking adventure and romance
in the mystical land of the pharaohs...

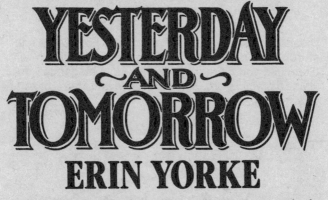

YESTERDAY ~AND~ TOMORROW

ERIN YORKE

A young British archeologist, Cassandra Baratowa, embarks
on an adventurous romp through Egypt in search of Queen
Nefertiti's tomb—and discovers the love of her life!
